QU_. __

Ella Vega

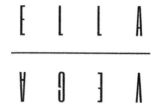

ELLA VEGA

This book may be ordered through booksellers or by contacting:

Ella Vega

4048 W Danby Ct
Winter Springs, FL
32708

ellavegaauthor@gmail.com

www.ella-vega.com

407.402.1832

ISBN: 979-8-2180-4861-7

Library of Congress Control Number: 2022914438

To Sam,
May life bring you friends like Kevin
and a love like Iris.

ELLA VEGA

CHAPTER I

I read the news today, oh boy...

There are times when life feels like a car crash. An average trip, and suddenly a loudness. Then hell breaks loose, unexpectedly, by which I mean life didn't ask for my opinion on the matter.

Life didn't ask me if I was ready for it. I don't recall signing any documentation before being born, transferring all rights to destiny's capricious aleatoricisim. And yet, here I was, staring at a wall like it was the grandest pleasure, drenched coat included in my scene. After all, rainy days are best for regret, not that life asked me my mood to graciously match it to the weather conditions. Just when you feel a fall in an abyss of self-pettiness, right before you start that inner phobophobia cycle of self-induced cardiac arrest and paranoia, some random act distracts you, thankfully.

"Excuse me?" a young woman whispers, as if she knew disturbing me was a necessary evil.

I turned my head around, my body too lazy to follow. My fists were still closed, grasping the infuriating notion of a forever missed opportunity.

"Yes?" My tone wasn't exceptionally evil. It wasn't her fault, after all. Still, she noticed my unnatural effort.

"Your phone is ringing," she said.

I'm pretty sure she meant: *snap out of it, for your own sake,* or *Are you ok? You seem to have witnessed a supernatural phenomenon,* but hey, we are all trying to be normal here.

"Yes, thank you,"

"Hello? "I answered, uninterested, pretending life was a gentle friend who keeps a record of its curved balls, balancing things out. In reality, life wasn't my friend that day, and I was naively looking at yet another disappointment around the corner.

As reluctantly predicted, I heard the sound of a familiar voice on the phone. It was my brother Renzo. He asked me how I was doing with a burdensome tone, the type of courteous talk that's superficial in nature. He was just waiting for me to be done with my answer, and I was waiting for him to state his business with me. I don't recall him ever being interested in my day or well-being. He didn't call unpretentiously or out of concern. I don't know if he was just practical on his phone use or deficient at social interaction.

"Now is not a good time, Renzo. I had an awful day, I'm soaking wet, and I just got laid off."

I knew he didn't care. I knew he wouldn't ask about it or be concerned about my failures. Still, I needed to vent, regardless of how important it was for him to know about my life or how the family gossip went down once he told Mom.

"Really?" he said.

Now, that did turn on every single alarm in my mental system. My palms, now relaxed from forgetting my previous ordeal, were suddenly sweating the weightful agony of Renzo's answer. I found the need to press my throat to release a big gulp of nothingness.

"What's wrong?" I said.

I continued to open my mailbox in that dingy first floor of my apartment complex. *"It has so much charm!"* people admired when asking for their opinion on the building. Now, it was just aged functionality merged with sanitation issues. New York was funny that way; the world sees a romanticized version of an old city whose better days don't seem to be ahead. Maybe it's just me, depressed from rushing every single day to perform like a circus clown. Maybe tourists did see a beautiful landscape that already expired in me. As I tried to get the mail, my sweaty hands deceived me. Some of my letters, or more accurately, bills, fell to the ground; if I could only manage to convince that outdated floor to swallow them whole!

"Let me help you with that," said the now known nosy helper, who had disappeared into the white noise of my current affairs just a minute ago. She was right there, picking up her mail, logically already looking at me as a mental patient. I looked at her and genuinely smiled at her perseverance. After all, heroes didn't get paid enough in the real world.

I finally noticed her. She was a young, carefree soul in the middle of a cynical Brooklyn block. Petite body type, but with some sort of greatness emanating from her personality. Hard to forget. No time for that little sunshine of a person. My thoughts went back to my brother's call.

"Renzo, you're scaring me," I said in my defense.

"Is everything okay?"

There was a considerable pause. This was an abnormal conversation by any standard, and I knew the topic would be less pleasant than my boss firing me this morning.

"Mom had an accident; she's in the hospital," Renzo continued,

"The hospital has my Costa Rican phone number as her emergency contact."

I took a deep breath. Not a cliché inhaling, but the type that breaks every second, like a lung after years of tobacco use. It wasn't an unhealthy habit that was keeping me from breathing properly. Life can do that to you.

His words were as gentle and composed as a different creature governing my brother altogether: he was calm, collected, attentive... This sober experience had already changed him, and it was just starting. I wondered what the end product of the story would be. Maybe he was going to become a better person. The same traumatic experience can be lived unbelievably different, depending on the person, at least that's what one of my old college professors used to say.

"Lucca?" he said, after anxiously waiting for a

couple of seconds.

"I can't go myself. If I get out of the country, I can't get back in."

The whole family feared my brother's immigration status. Legal immigration was a tedious and lengthy process. Even poverty was mandatory, I dare to say. With no visa to work, my brother, an advertising wizard and a million-dollar salesman for his previous employer, has resorted to charity to live in a country that he adopted as his own, just like me. This sort of experience traumatizes you. It creates some odd brain connections, leaving you with strange habits and deductions of life's patterns. You learn how to hoard, fearing another wave of scarcity. It sends a danger signal to your brain during times when you're supposed to be giving and selfless. People didn't understand, though. They just saw a guy unwilling to help, immediately assuming I had the strength to give. They were in their right, I suppose. After all, I had always been the hard-headed of the family.

I was trying to swallow the grave news. The whole world started spinning; my heart was beating fast. I felt a terrible lack of breath. The uncertainty of my mother's accident was creating physical evidence of a psychological scar. My hands were now cold from the experience. My mind had reached a limit. Suddenly I heard a loud and cheerful voice...

"Yes!" I heard the girl blissfully say to herself, without a care in the world.

It's funny how at the same moment in time, in such a reduced physical space, all kinds of people are gladly, regretfully, or tearfully receiving their respective news. Nothing controllable about it; it just is, like raindrops that fell on my now damp coat or snowflakes that were about to drop this coming winter. My eyes followed her as she disappeared into the stairs leading to the second floor. I took a deep breath, composed myself, and made a conscious decision to become the problem solver in the conversation. Not long ago, I was unequivocally the one singing jeremiads after bad news. But after a dozen books on the advantages of positive thinking, I successfully rewired my brain to be a little bit more forgiving towards life. Or so I thought.

"Tell me how serious it is and what happened," I bravely declared to my younger brother. I was hiding the massive tension headache behind those words.

Renzo explained the catastrophic accident to me. Mom, who was well in her 60s, still believed she was 25. She rode a motorcycle every day to run her errands. It was comfortable to ride a bike in a tropical coastal town—the wind is your ally when the weather is hot. Besides, it's the local predilection amongst the residents of Quepos. But those luxurious mountains full of wild natural beauty are traps for any commuter, local or foreign. The roads are narrow and curved, filled with blind spots and unpredictable traffic. Sometimes semitrailer truckers ignore the double yellow line to get ahead of their schedule, when they feel annoyed enough about the slow-paced tourists. The latter are too busy eyeing the monkeys and macaws instead of the road. They tend to want to stop, but the restrictive winding roads have a very marginal shoulder, leaving safety to the most distracted driver in this commotion of cars. It doesn't matter if you mind your own business or if you're a defensive driver. Things can go south by just a trucker's blood boiling enough to consider an illegality a necessity. As predicted by myself, when I insisted on the detriments of driving that white, second-hand Vespa, it was too dangerous for a senior to be "living the life" in such an exposed ride.

Right after the famous El Avión Restaurant, Mom saw a slow-moving car followed by the usual semi-truck. The truck was loaded heavily with palm harvest, which made the driver have a more challenging time speeding and stopping all the same. The 90s Toyota in front of the semi was going extraordinarily slow, probably deciding on dinner plans. The sun was setting, and mosquitos were already attacking my mother fervently. She was rushing to get home, the semi was hurrying to arrive at the processing plant, and the tourist was clueless about how dangerous his behavior was. The trucker accelerated to pass the car. My mother, oblivious, was too concerned about her lack of mosquito repellent. She was a cautious driver; no misunderstanding there. After all, there was a valid reason why mosquitoes could make a stop on her skin. The old Vespa didn't allow for rapid speed. That was one of the reasons I yielded my opposition to its purchase. Anyway, the mixture of circumstances created the perfect storm: the trucker assumed there was no one coming, and the cliff was just too steep on her side of the road to throw herself towards land. The result: my mother crashing head-on against the heaviness of a fully loaded truck. She was now unconscious, with a broken hip, broken arms, and a possible concussion pending doctor's confirmation. It didn't look good at all, even though Costa Rica had caring and knowledgeable doctors. *"The most permanent thing in life is change"* was one of her mottos while growing up. Well, life had undoubtedly proven her point.

"She's at the Max Terán Valls Hospital," my brother concluded, voice breaking to sorrow. I didn't want to participate in his premeditated elegy; I was too sensitive for that. I wouldn't be able to get out of the pessimistic scenarios in my head.

"Let me make inquiries and purchase the tickets; I'll call you back in a bit," I told him, feeling the resolve to hang up and call hospitals and acquaintances.

I needed to hear it from them for it to be real. So far, my mind played it like a story and not a fact. I guess that's what people call disbelief.

CHAPTER II

I'm leaving on a jet plane...

That night it was impossible to catch any sleep. My mind kept turning my stomach into my nemesis. All the nerves and news from that day were too much to handle. I turned and twisted around my Ikea-looking bed like a toddler. Anguish had me consistently visiting every corner of my bed. My ears wouldn't shut to everyday noises: the unrepaired sink dripping drop after drop, the air conditioning vent's sporadic rumble. My skin became a beast of its own, itching, reminding me it was there. My throat felt the bitterness of life's taste when things go wrong. I finally gave up on the disingenuous idea of a good night's sleep and grabbed my phone to ask for advice, as I usually did, except the person I talked to about such things was in the hospital, unconscious, for God knew how long. I stopped my chain of thought to avoid complaining about my mother's situation— we could still count on her to recover, after all. She wasn't forever lost; there was still hope.

I put the phone back on my nightstand and headed to the computer, feeling a sense of failure about the psychological comfort I was in dire need of. It was a cold early morning when I decided to purchase the airfare tickets. There it was: JetBlue flight 901 to San José, stopping at Orlando International Airport that night at 8 o'clock. I filled out all my information, and voilà, I was on my way to Quepos, Costa Rica. I rested my tense back against the chair and stared at the computer screen. I felt awfully concerned about the whole situation with Mom; she was living a full life, jumping from one beach to another in her little Vespa, enjoying herself. Now we didn't know what would happen to her; if she wasn't independent anymore, it would devastate her. How could she drive around and savor life the way she always had if she required constant help because of a sudden disability?

I tried to snap out of the ifs in life. They don't serve a purpose but to make sure you don't live in the present. After all, how good can it be to use your creativity to develop invisible scenarios that you scandalously react to? They're usually worst-case anyway. I never saw people happy about a current damaging affair, thinking it might turn out to be the greatest thing. Ifs are useless and petty. Nope! We aren't going to take that route anymore.

I decided to pack my bags, check for clothes that needed washing, find out what I needed to discard from the refrigerator. I used the rest of the day to prepare for a long trip. Maybe I'd get those Slushies Mom loved so much to keep her in good spirits when she woke up. I set a reminder to call my brother to get his homesick list; you know, cravings you couldn't find anywhere but in a foreign market.

If it wasn't a catastrophic event making me travel, one could think it was a good time of the year for it. You're avoiding high season, so beaches are going to be deserted. Locals will be open to plans and willing to help, more than the usual friendly advice typical of Costa Ricans. Even though I just lost my job, which suddenly became a foolish and shallow situation after my mom's news, I had enough cash to sustain myself for a good four weeks without a worry. I was mentally ready to be helpful, supportive. I was also detached enough from responsibilities to be off-radar. I was probably going to be busy visiting the hospital during the mornings, but the hospital's schedule wasn't going to allow me to be there outside visiting hours.

I headed out the door for a busy day of errands, secretly hoping that, at the end of this trip, I would have a sense of normality. I didn't need breakfast though; my stomach wasn't compatible with my emotions just yet.

As I headed downstairs, I notice the nosy helper closing her apartment door. This was the second time in my life I saw her. She was probably new to the building or one of those AirBnbs. Her enthusiasm was infectious, so I felt drawn to introduce myself. Honestly, my apartment was going to be unoccupied for so long that I felt the need to have a responsible neighbor know the situation, and she seemed to be up for the task.

"Hello again!" I greeted her from the hall as I walked closer, swinging my arms, my hands in my pocket,my coat moving back and forth. If one wants to appeal to a positive person, one should try to mimic positive behavior.

"Oh! The mail dropper! Hi! How was everything yesterday? You appeared to have had a rough day," she replied with a quirky tone and a friendly smile. By the look in her eyes, you could tell she was still trying to figure me out.

"Yeah, hard day..." I paused. She seemed to be the therapist type, but I wasn't about to explain my personal life to a perfect stranger. She also looked curious, so I felt she would ask questions, and I would hate to lie just to keep myself from sharing. I felt a particular pride in keeping myself honest. One day, someone would value that veraciousness in me, but that also put me in the particular position of explaining the reality of things in conversations instead of a simple lie to avoid sharing what was so deeply troubling me. It could potentially become burdensome under the wrong person's emotions and pretenses.

"Just wanted to thank you for helping me out yesterday and to introduce myself. My name is Lucca, your name is?" I cleverly asked her, persuing my anonymity in life. Maybe she wouldn't ask about yesterday's ordeal anymore. Maybe her eagerness to socialize wasn't intended particularly to me, but instead it was a personality trait. Maybe she was from a small town, where people were friendly by permeating one's privacy with such intrusions. Either way, I didn't perceive it as a weakness in character.

"Hey there, Lucca! You are officially my first acquaintance here in New York, apart from my friend Amanda. I'm Iris."

"Nice meeting you, Iris. Hopefully, we will become better acquainted soon. Anyway, are you new to the building or just visiting?" I continued, didn't want her to feel awkward about her concern. Caring people are worth respecting and hard to find.

"I just moved to Brooklyn to work at a clinic as an intern. My roommate is a good friend of mine and offered me one of her rooms," she replied.

She was easy to talk to. I couldn't figure her out, though. She seemed unpretentious and unchanged by life. That behavior, by itself, deserved my admiration. But I was on a mission; I needed a watchdog for my cave, so I proceeded to ask:

"I was wondering if maybe you could keep an eye on my apartment for a while. I need to travel urgently, and I couldn't make plans so close to my traveling date." I might have been too straight forward in asking for such a favor to a new acquaintance but I was desperate and out of options.

She immediately gestured a playful but sad look while squinting her eyes.

"Well, you see, Lucca," she explained with the most animated mannerisms coming from her small hands and figure. Her hands spoke by themselves. Small as they were, a fraction of mine, she said so much with them. She didn't have the type of gestures that suggested shallow thinking or a Disney princess copycat, but motions gentle enough to look real and friendly. She kept playing with her feet, as to be on her tippy-toes, swinging back and forth. She also had small feet, apparent by the size of her blue converse sneakers.

"I would have said yes just yesterday, but I received some fantastic news from a non-profit I applied for as a volunteer early in the year. They confirmed I'm clear to do my internship in Costa Rica! I'm so happy I get to travel... Anyway; I'm sorry I can't help you watch over your apartment. I can ask Amanda, see if she's available," she explained while also looking for her keys.

How odd! Suddenly, I had more in common with a perfect stranger than my with my neighbor Amanda, who appeared to be nothing but an abid coffee drinker to the point of nerve wreck. I'd met Amanda before, but she was a girl focused on herself and with a goal in mind, and God forbid an intrusion in her thoughts. Now I was traveling to my home-country, while my neighbor was going to a humanitarian mission to Costa Rica too.

People give the impression of loving Costa Rica. They tend to believe it's an eternal vacation spot where nothing absurd or harmful ever happens. The older generation flocks there because of its health care system and prices. People don't understand that when a first-world country person moves to a place like Costa Rica, prices go up for the local population to the point where we have to migrate to a different area altogether. The combination of corruption and inflation leaves locals with few options. My brother and I had the privilege of being raised in the private education system, so we could aim at scholarships due to our level of english, and thus, higher-paying jobs. I was the lucky one. I was hired by ADX as soon as I finished college here in New York. The company was impressed by my work, so they processed my visa but it was hard to start from scratch. I saw my classmates in college have better opportunities (and money) than myself. After graduating from a private school in San Jose, where I was considered privileged, I became part of the low-income class here in the U.S. The world is not a fair place by any means, and there's nothing better than a change in social class to give you a dose of reality. I tried not to be bothered by it, but my competitive spirit toyed with my mind and disabled my conscience.

"Seems like a fantastic opportunity!" I said to her. She was bubbly and smiling as if my congratulations were the next best thing. I felt like an absolute hero after she reacted in such a way. It's lovely to see how words can make someone's day. It helps people erase whatever tainted memory still preyed on their brain. Enough bad memories and eventually a person gets depressed. Acknowledging other people's victories seems like a scarce activity nowadays. Many people are policing, keeping tab of someone else's transgressions instead of their own. Giving encouragement helps destinity's scale balance out, instead of flipping one's mind towards the absolute chaos and negativity.

"Thanks! I always wanted to go there! My parents went decades ago, and they remember the place dearly. Maybe I'll also have a great experience to tell one day," Iris replied while opening her apartment door.

I applauded her aspirations and said goodbye. I genuinely felt happy for her. There are moments in life where the stars align, and you seem to think the world is in your hands. She was experiencing that moment of achievement in life. I'd bet if she asked Amanda anything, she'd say yes, so I agreed to her offer.

Off I went to the market. Part of living in America as an immigrant is becoming a mandatory courier for the entire family abroad. Your uncles, aunts, your mother's neighbors... everyone is desperate for some good that can be found in America for a lower price. Prices in Costa Rica are doubled with taxes, and salaries are considerably less than in America. So, whenever I can afford to pay for luggage, I also tried to bring some necessary goods to Costa Rica... Multivitamins for my uncle, some airy blouses and lipstick for my mother, eyedrops for the neighbor, and some brand sneakers from the discounted store for resale.

As I headed out, I thought about how fortunate I was to be available. Still, my mind knowingly chose to think about my reality and my problems. Having a sick parent is by no means a walk in the park, but having the health to help out is remarkable. I couldn't even imagine how Renzo was dealing with my mother's situation. Guilt might take over him because he didn't visit her. He might even be more consumed in his thoughts than myself, given the fact that he can't do much to help out but to wait for news. So I did count my blessings and felt gratitude towards life's opportunity to be available to the one person that had always been there for me. My conscience was clear; my anxiety, not so much.

CHAPTER III

Life is Life

It was boarding time at JFK. I was finally able to swallow some food after suffocating in a day that left me gasping for air. I had my headset on and my hands busy with all my belongings. I usually sat on the floor, at the closest corner to the boarding entrance. I was lying low, finally in sleeping mode, when I heard the boarding call for my flight; so I picked up and went to the boarding entrance. As I walked inside the plane to my seat, I got mentally ready to leave. You see, it wasn't just leaving, or visiting; it was also the unfamiliar situation that I was going to find myself in once I arrived. For the last several winters I'd visited Costa Rica, it had always felt like a vacation. A predictable vacation; a resting place. I usually arrived at a house full of my favorite food and a mother who was always willing to make everyone laugh. Now it was going to be me, trying to put up a fight against life's unpredictabilities.

The plane ride was turbulent, just like my

current situation. How fitting. Once I arrived, I headed to customs, which was easy if you have little luggage. Families with Costa Rican passports don't have it easy, though. They carry so many pieces of luggage. Remember what I told you about errands and goods that I should bring to my friends and family? Well, everyone does exactly the same thing, as much as they can. The government knows that, so they make sure Costa Ricans are just bringing what they consider their personal shopping, and not enough goods for resale. If they see a suspicious amount of purchases, they ban you from bringing anything else into the country for a certain period of time. Thank God it wasn't my case, since I only got one piece of luggage filled halfway with used clothes and shoes. It still felt uneasy going through customs, though.

Out I went into my second home: perfect weather, as always. The first thing in sight was a sea of orange cabs marking their hard-earned territory (God forbid they see an Uber or a red taxi, they have gotten physical before for this). My mom always reminded me NOT to take the orange cabs all the way to Quepos; they were costly compared to other cabs. Why? Well, the government decided those are the only cabs allowed to pick up passengers at the airport. So I took an orange taxi to the Mall Internacional, the closest mall to the airport, and from there I could find a more affordable ride to Quepos.

November is the end of the rainy season in Costa Rica. Subsequently, December carries a beautiful breeze and unforgettable sunsets. The lush greenery and the blue sky turn into a purple and pink explosion of color. This time tough, the trip from San José to Quepos was pitch black since it was late at night. Nevertheless, I had these sunsets engraved in my memory; they were my safe space during difficult times. Now I found myself in the middle of a trial, in the one place where everything was meant to be perfect. How paradoxical of life.

I tried ordering an Uber ride to Quepos, as it was way too late to ride a bus, and I wasn't in the mood to stay in a random hotel. It was hard to find a driver mad enough to pull an all-nighter though, especially when driving on the country's most dangerous highway. No driver will do that, partly because it's contrary to the Costa Rican way of life. "Pura Vida" or "pure life" is the country's slogan and motto. Costa Ricans, or Ticos, use it as a salutation or with an ironic tone to complain life is not great at the moment. They use it to state that food tastes good or to describe someone as a nice person. You can use it when someone doesn't behave as expectedly (with a sarcastic tone, obviously), or when you agree with the terms of a plan. It's quite the philosophy, really. Most of all, it means to live life to the fullest. It implies that fulfillment in life is about enjoyment and not about belonging to a big production machine. It means that if I'm a cab driver, I won't drive to Quepos at midnight for the sake of money.

There are good and bad aspects about the "Pura Vida" attitude. Everything sounds charming until you're hit with a wall of government incompetence, with employees that leave their desks at 4 o'clock because it's getting late. Or when no bank processes a loan during the month of December because it's Christmas and no one works. In summary, Pura Vida is excellent for tourists that want to relax and enjoy life, but for day-to-day obligations, it creates more stress and anxiety than merely doing what's required at your own retriment once in a while. Lucky for me, I know a guy... yes, contacts are essential in a small country. People wouldn't drive you four hours for money, but they would if they owed you a favor. That was why I brought all those brand name t-shirts I purchased at the outlet store. Kevin, my second cousin from my mother's side, knows. He was an Uber driver after hours. I also happened to know he was experiencing difficulties in his marriage and was willing to drive away, especially if it involved paid gas, a free brand t-shirt, and free stay at the most fantastic beach in Costa Rica. So I called him, and obviously, he told his wife it was a family emergency, and he had to leave for a couple of days.

"Hey, Kevin! Pura Vida!" I greeted Kevin, who seemed to enjoy practicing his English every time we met.

Kevin was quite the smart individual, and looked the part too. His Asian descent and thin black glasses filled up every stereotypical mind ever to justify the "smart Asian" idea. He was a lawyer during the day, but like many Costa Ricans, he had a hard time paying the bills with just one job, so he resorted to Uber driving during the evenings. He had a cool, tempered voice and deep sight. His father's side of the family also blessed him with darker skin, so the dude looked like a supermodel who decided to go to college.

"Mae! How are you! Good to see your face around this part of the world!" said Kevin.

Mae is another word for man in Costa Rica. It's pronounced "mah·eh" and is reminiscent to an age old joke of calling another person stupid as a nickname. To call someone stupid in the Tico culture is the worst spit on the face one can imagine. Everyone is smart. Even the neighborhood barber can make sense of any given subject. They are well-cultured people, understanding of the world around them and believers of healthy social interaction. Even though the word *Mae* started as a terrible insult, it was adopted culturally and ended up being the single most used word in the Tico language.

"Hey, Kevin! Nice to see you again! Thanks for coming so late and on such short notice."

"What did you bring from the Big Apple?" he immediately asked, already thinking about his form of payment.

"A brand-name T-shirt?" I suggested, bartering for a ride.

"No way! It's four hours, man!" He laughed but refused. He turned his face around as if he was psychologically already regreting the deal.

"What shoe size are you?" I asked him, gauging his feet through the darkness of the car.

"Ten and a half?" he said with a smile.

"Nike?" I cleverly suggested, knowing he was going to be happy about the trade.

"Now we're talking!" he said while rubbing his hands together. He changed the gear of the car and accelerated, sealing the deal.

"Thanks, really," I emphasized to him, graving his bicep as to make him understand it was a serious expression. He could have very well gotten out of the deal easily, if he wanted to.

"No worries! I'm happier here than anywhere else! Especially on a Friday night!" he said, laughing ironically. He was obviously refering to his current family dynamic, which was making him uneasy to say the least.

There is no such thing as secrets in my family. Everyone talks about every little detail with everyone else, and we all know. It's such a burden when one wants to be discreet, but when help is needed, your cousin comes to pick you up at midnight and drives you four hours to your destination.

As we drove, we bantered for hours about world affairs and the difference in perception with our respective home countries. We discussed the gloomy economic conditions in Costa Rica and the tense political atmosphere in the U.S. We talked about his personal issues with his wife, and how unsolvable they were. We discussed my mother's accident and her current medical report. He reminded me that his brother was working in the same hospital where Mom was, and how he could update me whenever he passed by her bed. We talked until we eventually zoned out and felt uninterested and tired of solving the world.

On our way to Quepos, first we went through Jacó, the closest beach to San José, the capital city. Jacó has several beaches around, and its waves are big enough for a weekend of surf. It has a hidden beach–not so hidden from the locals–called *Playa Blanca* or White Beach. It is the closest white sand beach from San José, and it has suitable public areas. It was my favorite place as a child. It was close enough for my inner voice to hold the "are we there yet" age-old question and far enough to consider it a vacation destination.

After driving through Jacó, it all became a blur of dreams. My sleepy head found a way to use my New Yorker winter coat as a pillow on top of my seat belt. I was deep in my dream, when suddenly I heard a horrible screechy sound, followed by a sudden movement that threw my body out of position and into concern. I opened my eyes and looked at Kevin, who was staring at me, pale as a ghost. His glasses, now on top of my leg, were twisted. My backpack, which was previously unzipped and left open, was now on my lap, its contents all over me. The opened apple juice previously placed in between seats, was spilled all over Kevin's right thigh.

"What just happened?" I demanded, staring at Kevin.

Kevin, already reacting to the scene, pulled to the shoulder of the road to gain composure and fix his glasses. He took three consecutive breaths before explaining.

"I think the driver in front of us got increasingly drunker. We've been behind that same car for the past hour, but his driving got lethargic enough to almost provoke an accident just now," Kevin said with a broken voice full of anger and fear. He pointed at an old Jeep Sahara also on the shoulder of the road, but in a different direction.

Out of the car came a young man rocking and laughing with his peers, who were still inside the vehicle. A second person came out, went around the front of the vehicle with an obstinate walk, arms swinging full force. They appeared to be both disgruntled and amused, I guess depending on the level of alcohol abuse.

"Let's leave them alone," stressed Kevin.

"We don't know what their reaction is going to be."

Kevin got out of the car to shake the juice off his pants, now soaking. It was no use, he was a wet mess. He walked to the trunk and grabbed some shorts from my luggage.

"Do you mind?!" he yelled at me, already taking his pants off in the middle of the road. I looked through the old mirror and noticed he grabbed a pair of my denim shorts.

"Go ahead!"

He came back in after replacing his outfit and proceeded to change the car's gear, determined to finish his trip more cautiously and smoothly.

That was when it sank in. My mother experienced the same situation, but she was alone, and a truck hit her badly enough to leave her unconscious. I couldn't even imagine how terrifying it would have been. She undoubtedly saw everything in slow motion with the unstoppable outcome that came to be. She probably had all these thoughts in her head, seconds before the truck impacted her. Possibly fear overwhelmed her mind and body right before falling motionless on the road. It rages my conscience to know that an ill-mannered driver can end someone's life for his own sake. Just like the drunk driver who almost provoked an accident.

Kevin and I were quiet for a while after the incident. I couldn't sleep, thinking that maybe Kevin needed another set of eyes to help him be aware of his surroundings. It was late, and he needed someone to help him stay awake. So we turned the radio on and headed south. Apparently, life insisted on letting me know it doesn't take breaks.

CHAPTER IV

Listen, do you want to know a secret?

T he midday heat woke me from my deep sleep. I hadn't slept soundly for days, and my mind finally settled in the persistent thought that I couldn't control it all. Maybe life is meant to be a teacher and not a friend. Perhaps we're on this earth to experience defeat and see what we choose to think. Who knows what we're meant to believe.

Yesterday culminated in a safe arrival home. We reached our destination at 4 a.m. Insects were chirring and frogs were still croaking while we got our luggage out of the car and headed to Mom's house. Her keys were easy to find—always on the window sill next to the carport. Her private guard, Ed, spotted us and opened the gate. He was probably expecting someone already after Renzo called him. The gate itself was a massive wrought iron dual swing beauty, held by two rectangular concrete posts. The posts were seven feet high and crowned by two lines of terracotta bricks. An old buganvillea plant embraced the gate like an old friend's hug. Its fuscia flowers contrasted against the white wall as if nature itself was vain enough to dress up for my arrival. Its spells were useless under the darkness of the night, and all its glory was just a memory. On one side of the gate there was a gatekeeper's house, which shared a wall with the perimeter of the property. This wall, right next to the post, created a proper space for the farm name: "El Retoño" or "The Offspring". The rest of the property had a perimeter fence created by old posts and wire, nothing that would stop an unwelcome intruder. No one would dare to enter through, since the land was surrounded by another property that included mountains of rainforest and rivers.

The next day I woke to the birds singing, letting me know it was time to get up. I found myself contemplating the cedar ceiling of my bedroom, with a rhythmic interruption performed by the ceiling fan. My mom's house was a traditional Costa Rican home. A one-story ranch with gorgeous wood ceilings and white, stucco walls inside out. Costa Rican houses tend to have wood everywhere; not long ago, plastic was a luxurious commodity, and trees were the local, more abundant option. The house, crowned with its traditional roof tile, painted a quaint landscape upon arrival to the property, particularly due to its round tile rooftop and vegetation.

I got up due to the stickiness of my own sweat on the bedsheets. I stretched well enough to feel I could tackle the hasty day ahead; reaching headboard and footboard as fervently as a traveler's last goodbye before leaving a loved one. The window in my room faced a balcony, and it had a remarkable view of the local hills. It was big enough to fit me sitting down on its sill, so I ventured out for the sake of old times. The window, a little stuck from age, gave me a chance to slow down and appreciate the immense view: mountains as far as the eye could see, with uncontrollable, almost hysterical flora hanging from every tree, branch, and leaf. Macaws flew in groups of two from one area to another, disappearing into the landscape. As I took a breath, I felt that the greenery took all my troubles away, turning them into trivialities. Suddenly the previous night's ordeal wasn't an issue, my mom was going to recover, and my job would be waiting for me when I went back to New York.

My stomach rumbled, so I headed back inside to get some breakfast.

"Hey, Kevin!" I yelled, assuming my cousin was awake and ready to eat. But there was no answer. So I headed to the kitchen to seek what Mom left behind before the unthinkable happened. A rancid smell, almost as if a dead animal perished inside days before, emanated from the kitchen.The milk was spoiled. The orange juice smelled gruesome. The worst scent came from the trash can, revealing putrified meat and worms, characteristic of tropical weather waste.

"What is there to eat?" I thought to myself while closing the trash bag to put it out for removal. Then a wire chicken surfaced in the corner of my eyes, brown eggs futilely hiding inside. "Eggs it is." I was about to turn the stove on, when suddenly the phone rang.

"Hello?" I answered.

"Hi, Lucca, how was the trip?"

"Renzo! Good, a little too eventful for my taste, but alive and well."

"Listen, I called the hospital to ask about visiting hours and information on Mom," Renzo replied. There was a pause between our easygoing conversation.

I was already aware that Mom was in a delicate condition, but I wouldn't guess how bad it was until I saw her in person.

"Lucca, Mom was transferred to the ICU," Renzo continued urgently.

I couldn't hear a thing after that statement. A ringing in my ears interrupted. My vision turned a bit blurry, and my stomach became a beast of its own, painfully reminding me that I was still alive. I couldn't take it anymore. As tears started to fall down my cheeks, my brother and I came to the revelatory conclusion that we would end up being each other's exclusive family one day. Some time from now, we were only going to have each other. There was no one left. Dad died years ago from cancer; there were no more brothers, sisters, or partners. I realized I was alone. I hadn't made time for relationships, and it had proven lonely in the long run. Focusing on myself had brought to my attention that I was going to stay by myself if I didn't change course. I cried. My thoughts were too overwhelming.

As I reevaluated my life, I sat on the floor, fighting for air. The cold floor didn't seem to be a problem for my bare skin. The patterned encaustic tile, with its crowded black and white circles product of my tears, looked like bubbles that once flew free from bursting and dying, only to find themselves trapped by gravity. It became a literal explanation of how life always brought me back to my knees, even when I thought nothing else could go wrong. I needed to vent my troubles away, and today was that day. I wasn't angry, though. I didn't feel the need to punch a wall, or break glass, like the characters in a dramatic movie scene. It wasn't about control or the lack of it. It was about the pain and loneliness that comes with the feeling that your last parent might not be on this earth for much longer.

Shortly after, there was a screeching noise that gradually became louder, followed by a blast. I ran to the hall, and there was Kevin, with a shocked face, holding on to a doorknob. He accidentally knocked down the old, malfunctioning door of the guestroom. The door fell on the last wood wall of the house, perforating a large hole in it. Looking back, the scene was quite comical. With his eyes wide-open, Kevin didn't know if he should react like a naughty child who just broke his mother's favorite vase; or like an accomplice who just got away with his mischievous deed. He was waiting for me to react. I was in a completely different world, trying to recover from deep feelings and tragic notions. I slowly got closer, trying to avoid dozens of wooden splinters from reaching my bare feet. There it was, a big, broken plank from the old siding of the house. The door only seemed to be mildly scratched, which didn't surprise me a bit. Every door in that old house was solid wood, almost as heavy as the semi-truck that hit mom.

"Help me move the door to the side!" said Kevin, already putting strength into action.

I quickly wiped my tears away and set the phone on one of the shelving units closest to the incident. I put my hands on the heavy door, and together we pulled it to rest on the adjacent wall. Now feeling a bit guilty about the accident, Kevin hurried to get a broom to clean the mess. I stared at the massive hole, feeling the need to introspect. The white siding had broken to show the wall's interior structure. If Mom were here, she would probably be mad at the incident, which damaged the only plank wall of the house. She loved that old wall, and when she built the new house, she was emphatic not to demolish any of it. Maybe it had some sort of sentimental value, since it was part of a previous structure. Nevertheless, the wreck revealed an interesting artifact: an old-looking tin box, resting inside the wall as a dormant dragon not to be disturbed.

"Hey, Kevin!" I called my cousin, rushing him to attend to my discovery.

"Look at that weird box inside the wall."

He quickly went to grab his glasses inside the guestroom. Kevin was the curious type, and he knew he didn't want to miss a tin box inside a wall. He carefully got closer to ground zero, almost tripping over the edge of the fallen door.

"It's probably a time capsule of some sort," I stated

with an almost childlike fascination.

I slowly tried to clean the debris on top of the box as if it were the most remarkable object. By then, Kevin was ready with his eyeglasses on and his mind already making a story about the findings. I was honestly just trying to keep my mom in my mind. Maybe it was her keepsake, and it would remind me of her.

I grabbed the box and walked between the debris to set my discovery on the coffee table in the living room. Kevin followed me swiftly. We both sat on the 70s-looking couch, contemplating the corroded tin that appeared to be of a golden color long ago. Its corners were green from the exposure to humidity, corroded from the environment it was stored in.

"I wonder why someone would've put a tin box inside a wall," asked Kevin, assuming it was a precarious place to hide an item; if that was the author's intent.

"That wall is the only remaining wall from the old house. The box is probably older than the new addition, which happened in the 70s," I informed Kevin, who was craving for the anecdote behind it as much as its contents.

The phone rang unexpectedly right in the middle of our intense unveiling. It was my brother

Renzo, who I was crying with minutes ago. He heard a bang; after the blast, I was too astonished and forgot to inform him of the ordeal.

"Renzo, I forgot to call you back. I'm sorry."

"Lucca, I called the hospital, you need to be there before 3 p.m., or they won't let you in." The sense of urgency made me jump from the couch to my room. Kevin also rushed to his room to change. We decided to leave our curious minds thirsty for a bit more and get ready to visit the hospital. Duty called, but frankly, I was in dire need of closure. Waiting is the worst battle a person may have. Doing something to solve an issue isn't nearly as hard, regardless of what it is. It was time to confront my fear; the terror of reality's starkness: my mother's unconscious body.

CHAPTER V

Livin' on a prayer

K evin and I arrived at the Max Terán Valls hospital 30 minutes after the door incident. It was a sunny day, unlike the gray concrete structure of the hospital. After finding a parking place and walking to the entrance, it was difficult to believe that an area so rich in flora would have such a rebellious gloomy structure. Nothing was impressive when it came to the hospital's façade; just a big, gray wall with concrete floor and concrete walls. Everything was gray and dull, almost screaming the melancholy of the patients buried under layers of hospital blankets and machinery.

As we approached the main entrance, a security guard greeted us and kindly asked for our admission cards.

"Admission cards?" I asked the guard, who seemed to pick an already foreign accent in my oral expression. After a certain amount of time of not visiting your native country, some sounds specific to your native tongue fade away until they become difficult to pronounce. My r was too rolled, I could tell. The security guard could also tell.

"Gringo? No worries! Just go to the admissions office to get a card to visit." He gave me the directions to get to the admissions department and instructions on how to get the card. I guess he was more a guide than an officer. He seemed to know every single process. He smiled and helped everyone around while making jokes with the lady who cleaned the entrance hall floors. I wanted to have that. I missed tremendously how ticos could become the best of friends with anyone who crossed their path. People laughed out loud everywhere, even under the most extreme circumstances, such as a hospital setting.

Kevin was busy with his phone while I was talking to the guard. By the time I headed to the admissions department, Kevin already had a different way in, not involving the admissions process or the main entrance.

"Lucca, remember about my brother who works here? He will take us in whenever we need through the staff entrance."

As scandalous as it sounds, it's common to access government hospitals with staff instead of through the front door. The culture in Costa Rica is different. People love to relate to each other through favors and helping out. Sometimes it leads to corruption, though, so I wasn't sure how to proceed.

I decided to go with Kevin's plan and get the admission card after today's visit. I didn't want to insult anyone by not accepting a favor, nor did I want to encourage such behavior outside an already maxed-out system. As we went through the staff door, I could see how people allowed themselves to express their minds without restraints. People were arguing about the current health system and politics from opposing sides. Seconds later, those same people were laughing about how inefficient everything was. Maybe I shouldn't take life so seriously. Perhaps I should allow myself to believe that strangers are agreeable and that they are good people.

As we arrived at one of the many doors of that hallway nightmare of a building, I saw a tiny body wrapped in turquoise-colored bed sheets. Her recognizable curly, gray hair told me right away I was looking at my mother. I couldn't see her face very well, from all the monitors and gadgets to help hospital staff keep her stable. As I got closer, I hesitated for a second. I didn't want to change the image I previously had of her: her strength, her active lifestyle, the jokes and laughter to break the ice; I didn't want to lose her essence. But life came knocking anyway, and I had to leave my thoughts of despair for another day. So off I went to be by her side. Kevin saw me struggling, so he laid his hand on my shoulder. He wanted to let me know I wasn't alone, but I saw myself in the middle of a lonely field in my thoughts.

"Let's take life as it is, and not as it should be," he said, trying to encourage me not to despair. It sounded like something out of a Hallmark card, but as patronizing as it was, he was right.

My mother's gesture said it all: she was unconscious, with her mouth wide open and her cheeks almost falling from her face. Her hands were oddly relaxed, and her small, chunky feet were cold as ice. I didn't know how to react. My mind tried to understand that she was the same person with more energy than me not even six months ago, when I saw her last. An unwanted tear fell on my cheek to remind me of my human experience. I looked down the floor to rest my mind from such a tragic scene, almost waiting for it to pass. I noticed that deep inside my soul, I had the option of choosing hope over fear. Of course, it's easier to be afraid; that's the natural, more animal instinct. But hope? That takes effort; a conscience. For hope to exist, it is necessary to rise above the situation.

"I know you, neighbor," whispered a familiar

voice, interrupting my transcendental chain of thoughts.

"Iris?" I asked out loud, with a doubtful tone and a secret desire to see her again. After all, it was a completely different scenario where I talked to her not long ago.

"Hey! How are you? And what are you doing with my patient?" Iris surprisingly said while smiling at me. Her black eyes described wisdom that understood what I was going through, but her lips uncovered a playful child who wanted to express empathetic sadness. I smiled back at her with melancholy still in my heart.

"Iris, this is my mom, Aura. She had a car accident. My brother called me right when I met you in New York." It's easier to be familiar with a person you hardly know when you are outside of your context. In New York, we're strangers. Here, in Costa Rica, we are two fellow New Yorkers with many things in common.

"I'm sorry to hear that... Lucca". She was struggling to remember my name. An understandable situation, given the fact that she just met me days ago.

"I'll make sure she has everything she needs while in my care," Iris replied while showing me a blanket she'd been holding. She opened the blanket and covered my mom with it, making sure her feet were well under the covers.

After a while, a taller woman arrived at the bedside. She was busy-looking, focusing on some paperwork at hand. She was Dr. Chang, the doctor in charge of the wing. She explained to us how delicate the situation was: her brain swollen to the point where a coma state was necessary for the sake of her well-being. Dr. Chang also described how her body was broken in different parts and educated us on the respective healing process. The information pictured a scene from a horror movie, not an experience my mother would go through.

"She's lucky to be alive," she emphasized with her chart pointing at me and her glasses well down her nose.

"She's in stable condition, and we believe she will recover once she overcomes the very dangerous swelling in her brain."

I wanted to ignore the *if* of the explanation she just gave me. I wished it was a challenging but absolute path to recovery instead. Regardless, it gave me a little hope. Once you have a goal in your mind, in this case, a milestone regarding her brain's swelling, I could imagine a better scenario.

I tried to give her my hand. She used to love the pronounced curve on my fingers. As a child,

I remember her teasing me by biting my fingers as if they were a banquet's delight. She used to pretend she would chew them and then swallow them with a big gulp, later telling me they were "yummy". Her hand was warm, reassuring me of her life still on this earth.

"Lucca, I'm here if you need anything," said Iris while putting her hand on my shoulder. Her nosy predisposition helped me get over my damming thoughts of an obscured future and a nostalgic past.

"I'm sorry about all of this," said Kevin. Both comforting words created a very supportive environment. I felt loved. It has been a long time since I last felt that awful sensation of an empty stomach going away in the middle of a difficult moment. There was always a feeling of falling down a roller coaster whenever I faced daunting circumstances. Maybe I just needed a support group. Perhaps we are not supposed to live life as individuals, but as a family, as a pack. We aren't eagles; we're wolves. An eagle lives alone and in the air. A wolf has a family, a leader who would give up their life to protect his pack when there's a threat.

"Thanks for the encouraging words, both of you. By the way, Kevin, this is Iris. She's my new neighbor. I met her back in Brooklyn."

Kevin fixed his glasses and greeted her. He

saw how I looked at Iris and decided to be so bold as to invite her to the beach to watch the sunset. I internally panicked and stared at him as I used to stare at my mother when, in my teens, she would share private information about me with one of her friends.

"Sure, that would be great! I'm out right after this round, and I don't know the area."

"Great! Let's meet at Manuel Antonio National Park," said Kevin in a persuasive manner.

"Isn't Manuel Antonio closed after four?" I asked, sure of the situation from quickly browsing the web.

"It is! Which means a friend of mine can let us in and have the beach all to ourselves!".

"I appear to be friends with a mobster," I teased him while Iris looked at us, lifting a brow.

"It's ok, man; he's a ranger, and part of his job is to do rounds at night. We're actually helping him by doing the 3km walk to the tip of the beach. They're understaffed, and I help once in a while, so I know the regulations. In exchange, I get to go see the sunset unsupervised."

I looked at Iris again for a sign of approval. Anything that would tell me I could be glad to go.

"Ok, I'll go, just because you volunteer, Kevin, and Lucca here is already a friend, right, Lucca?" She pointed at me and smiled. I couldn't help but smile back.

I looked at mom and stopped holding her hand as if she could approve or disapprove of my little trip through the use of telepathy. As I gazed at her, I saw a space between her hairline and the machinery on her face where I could kiss her forehead. So I went for it. I kissed her unapologetically like she used to do when I was running around full of sweat after soccer practice. I missed her dramatic reactions every time I expressed my affection or gave her undivided attention. I missed her voice when I called to say hi. I missed her rascal-looking smile whenever she got away with something.

"I won't promise everything would be as you want it to be in the future, but I can promise everything will be fine. Regardless of the situation, you're going to be fine," Iris replied, looking into my eyes. She declared absolute truth. That was it. I understood why people keep telling each other everything would be fine. You are going to be ok, regardless of the circumstances. You'll get over this. You can handle it.

"Hopefully." I chucked, understanding that her reality was very different from mine, very real nevertheless.

Kevin took his hand out of his pocket and waved bye to Iris. He hugged me like a gorilla climbing a tree right after she turned around. I wasn't used to that type of genuine physical affection anymore. I smirked at him. In reality, the ambiguity of the moment left me confused, to say the least.

We headed to the admissions office to get my visitation permit. After an hour or so of standing in line, I was able to get the bureaucratic piece of paper. I now knew why people shamelessly accessed the hospital through the staff entrance. "Tortuguismo" or turtling as they call it. The act of slow movement. No wonder we all need friends here in Costa Rica. I finally headed home to eat and rest before we saw the sunset at the beach.

CHAPTER VI

I still haven't found what I'm looking for...

Kevin and I arrived at "El Retoño" after our traumatizing visit to the hospital. While we were parking the car, we remembered the old tin box that got us so excited.

"Mae!" I called Kevin. The word *"mae"* has quite the story behind it. Gossip tells the tale of how, during the 1940s or so, there were a substantial amount of shoe stores in San Jose. They all sold leather shoes that needed staff to appropriately treat the leather by squeezing it against machinery. It was hard work that no one wanted to do, so the new employee, whoever it was, would always be the one squeezing or *"majando"* the leather. The other workers would laugh at the new person, telling them that they fell on the wrong job by saying they *"calló de maje"*. Eventually, they would call them *"maje"* instead of their name until they were promoted and some new fool would come to work and be the *"maje"*. The word *"maje"* eventually evolved to be just *"mae"*. And that's how every single person turned out to call each other a fool in Costa Rica.

"The tin box!" Kevin said, while falling into the excitement of our new venture.

"This deserves some take-out! I'm definitely not cooking!" he suggested, while grabbing his phone to call the closest take-out restaurant. I got out of the car and headed to the house to wait for Kevin.

As Kevin came in, I proceeded to open the little rusted box very gently. It's hard to find antiques in this part of the world. This tin box was quite the exception, and it definitely belonged to my family, who had owned this land for a while.

"Wait!" said Kevin, taking his phone out. He wanted to capture the moment we opened the box for posterity.

He quickly came to sit right next to me, jumping on top of an old, wood coffee table, landing right on the couch. As I opened the box, the first thing I saw was a two-page, faded, yellowish booklet. There was also a necklace in surprisingly good condition, a black-and-white picture of a man in uniform, a letter, and a small key. Kevin and I were both looking at the box with our mouths open, like those kids who found the game Jumanji in their basement.

I first grabbed the faded booklet for a closer look. The front cover had an insignia that read "C.C.S.S.", I opened the booklet, which contained personal information such as the birth date and place of birth. The name was ineligible, probably from everything the booklet had endured hidden in between walls. The last name was readable, but it didn't make sense; "of Prussia", the booklet stated. By the looks of it, he was already deceased...the booklet was issued in 1941. There was a section for a photograph, telling by the change of texture and color of the paper, already torn a bit by a third party. I passed the card to Kevin, who was already feeling like a child on Christmas Day.

"What do you think that is, Kevin?" My hand already on my chin as if rubbing it would magically bring new information to light.

"Look at that!" said Kevin, like one who sees an old toy from their mom's attic.

"What is it?"

"Give me your wallet, Lucca." I suspiciously agreed to the offer for the sake of my curiosity. He got my recently acquired admissions paperwork from the hospital and took it out, revealing identical acronyms and information. He pointed at the initials and said:

"C.C.S.S-Caja Costarricense de Seguro Social." Of course, "La Caja", as ticos call it, is a public entity in charge of offering free health care to both citizens and immigrants. Sounds all wonderful, until you realize that just to pay for this service, every able working person has to pay around 10% taxes coming off directly from the wages. This tax, added to the other impossible taxation on wages, comes to a total of almost 30% taxed income, plus taxes to purchases, property, etc. The service itself is terrible for routine checks and non-emergency procedures such as needed scheduled surgeries, but it is a life saver when it comes to emergencies and medication.

"So, the old booklet is actually an old admissions card?" I asked Kevin. After all, I left Costa Rica not fully aware of every single document issued by the government, nor did I know how historic documents looked like.

"Yes, it looks exactly like the one my grandma had. Mom kept it as a keepsake when she died; they look exactly the same," Kevin replied while fixing his glasses.

"I bet your mom has yours from when you were born, back in the day when people still wrote by hand or typed in typewriters." Kevin laughed, like he wasn't older than me.

"Dude, speak for yourself, I was born in 1990; you're the one who's already married."

Kevin kept laughing at his joke, omitting my magnificent comeback. With him, it wasn't about who won the conversation, or who had a point; it was about laughing out loud at life. Seems fitting if you ask me, a more appropriate way to live life. It multiplies the amount of good chemicals being released by one's brain, and knits closer relationships that in return will become lasting friendships. Maybe that was the key to the "pura vida" lifestyle that I so unintentionally forgot about after moving to New York: laughing at life, instead of crying about it. So I laughed too. He kept laughing, not a minute of awkwardness in between. Another Costa Rican trait that is key to happiness; if you don't get the other person, well... you ask what they mean! As simple as that. You don't assume they're crazy, or weird, or deserving of sarcastic looks. You understand, and if you don't, you communicate until you do. Blooming relationships are damaged the most from avoiding this practice: the typical strangers who talk to each other in a friendly way until one of them said something that made the other a bit uncomfortable. The other retreats, assuming the worst, in fear of what the person might have meant. And that's it. No love or good intentions. Just a wimpy and lazy attitude towards relationships whose road ends in loneliness.

After my stomach hurt and my eyes were tearful from laughing so hard, Kevin and I resolved to keep looking at the box. I grabbed the necklace and showed it to Kevin. It was thick and heavy, mostly metal, with some colorful incrustations. It was a very masculine looking piece, much like the ones you see in medieval movies. Hanging from the bottom was a larger part, an insignia, with a black eagle and a crown.

"That seems to be the official attire for drinking beer!" Kevin chuckled. And he was right. It looked exactly like the logo used for the local beer— *Imperial*. In between jokes, Kevin was proving to be a very good source of information. He put it on and indeed it was heavy and certainly not meant for a small body. I followed the joke by running into the kitchen to get some Imperial beer my mom kept for visitors and proceeded to take a picture of Kevin. He posed quite well, lowering his glasses and graving an ornamental cane from the living room.

I went back to the tin box–after high-fiving Kevin for our successful attempt at comedy–and took out the key. Small, yet heavy, the key seemed to belong to a vintage keyhole more than a practical, up-to-date use. So I put it in my pocket with the hopes of trying it in every possible keyhole.

"Let me see," argued Kevin, jealous of my discreet move. I handed the key to him as if he could tell me more about it. He looked at me and shrugged, as clueless as I was. Kevin handed the item back to me for safe keeping, so I put it back in my pocket.

Finally there was another piece of paper, also yellow due to age. A handwritten letter, impossible to read, but dearly treasured by whoever put it inside the tin box. Its cursive strokes and accumulation of ink on the curves of each letter told me it must have been the oldest item in the box, dating back to whenever ink was still sold in bottles and writing was as much an art as it was a luxury.

Since I was starting to feel exhaustion from stress and the afternoon laziness from the heat, I decided to take a break from the tin can adventure and went to nap for a bit, while Kevin turned on the TV and zoned out. Even though the earlier hours were nerve racking, it was all bearable. The laughs and goofiness from the afternoon were perfect medicine for my stress. *Someone gets to have the last laugh,* I thought, *If it's not you, then it's going to be life.*

CHAPTER VII

Hooked on a feeling

"Lucca! Lucca! Wake up!" I could hear Kevin's voice like a far cry.

"Lucca! Remember Iris? We have to go!" As I became aware of my thoughts from earlier during the day, I remembered my commitment to Iris. I woke as fast as I could to get ready. By ready, I mean I swiftly put on my swimsuit shorts and my sleeveless shirt. I also got my hat, sunscreen, mosquito repellent, and flip-flops. Kevin was already waiting for me in the car by the time I headed out. We drove to the entrance of Manuel Antonio National Park— my favorite beach in the entire country. The road was winding and full of vegetation on both sides. An incredible landscape, almost as if nature was screaming at us to look at her at every turn. I could easily see how Mom could make the wrong turn, though, or how a truck could have little visibility while trying to pass another vehicle.

The afternoon was fresh, so we decided to open our windows to feel the cool ocean breeze. The air had a salty scent due to our proximity to the sea. There was a variety of birds flying and singing. Their respective noises combined with the ocean waves made perfect music to my ears. Hearing the repetitive sounds of nature brings calm even to the most extenuating circumstances.

As we arrived at sea level, we noticed no traffic or street vendors, typical of the park's entrance during regular business hours. We arrived at the gate where Kevin stopped to ask for *"Chema"*. The gatekeeper smiled and asked if he was Kevin. After confirming our identity, he opened the gate entrance and let us in. We got inside and parked right to our left, close to the bathrooms. After around five minutes, another car arrived. Out came a familiar figure—a tiny woman with black hair, this time wearing a red swimsuit under a semi-transparent white dress. She was carrying a big red, beach bag, which seemed to hold her whole baggage load from New York. She approached the gate while Chema got her right in, probably from looking at us wave at her frantically.

"Hello, neighbor," Iris said, giving me a half-smile. That smile was simply too much for my heart not to race at a million heartbeats per second.

"Hey, Iris! How was your day?" I was about to

finish my sentence when stupid Kevin said:

"Oh, you have to kiss him." We both looked at him, red from embarrassment and clueless about the statement.

"You kiss people on the cheek here, you know, to greet them." Kevin smiled, not having a clue of the awkward moment he just imposed on both of us.

"Don't mind him, Iris. He's just teasing us." Kevin didn't get what he said until that very moment. He got a bit red and laughed like he always did whenever life brought discomfort.

"Here in Costa Rica, people kiss on the cheek to say hi, instead of the traditional handshake," I explained. Iris laughed at both of us.

"You boys are silly... Why do you care so much how I say hi? Kevin?" She seemed to not be uncomfortable at all, ironically reprimanding Kevin for his naive comment.

Kevin, still blushing, changed the conversation. Iris appeared to be doing just fine with his playful nature. Kevin proceeded to walk away, hurrying us up into the forest for the sake of a spectacular sunset.

"Impressive work," I whispered to her while walking away from the car. She looked at me and winked, almost as if she were having fun from such a tease.

We walked into the forest for quite a while, always fleeing the clouds of mosquitoes trying to have a feast out of us. Kevin became our guide, explaining the number of visitors the park receives every year. He pointed at where the hidden waterfalls were located and suggested we visit for a second time to dive into them. He explained to us about the trees' species, about the trails, and the different beaches accessible through the park. Iris was a nature lover and had a blast on the path to the beach. She took a thousand pictures: some of nature and us together, others of her, or just us two, and Kevin and me... She didn't even imagine the spectacle she was about to see.

As we got closer to the beach, we could see the trees clearing out, welcoming us to a breathtaking sky painted with blues. The sea, infinite and turquoise, touched the white sand so characteristic of Manuel Antonio. Behind us was the hysteric flora descending from the mountain, displaying itself in an array of greens. The air carried an unfamiliar petrichor to our curious noses. Manuel Antonio National Park is composed of a series of coves instead of a big beach, having the unintended effect of intimacy and privacy. We arrived at the main beach at 4:40 p.m. Iris took her bag out, or so I thought, which became a throw for everyone to sit on. It reminded me of my mom, who would put her beach throws on like a dress right before leaving the beach.

"So it wasn't just a purse?" I asked Iris with the hopes of starting a new conversation with her.

"I'm a very practical person, Lucca," replied Iris, while we both opened the throw and set it on the sand.

"In the medical profession, you can't afford to be impractical," emphasized Iris while smiling, out of pride or politeness; who knows.

By then, Kevin was already testing the water temperature, like it was going to be anything other than the average 80 degrees it always is.

"It's so good! You guys have to get in!" Kevin yelled while running back to us. Kevin quickly took off his shirt and threw it on the throw.

"Are you coming?" he asked, moving his chin up and taking off his glasses.

"I don't know, maybe."

Kevin, being the strong type he is, spontaneously lifted me up.

"What the hell are you doing?!" I shouted; an irrelevant gesture, since I was already on his shoulder, half of my body hanging upside down.

"I figured you would need a push… You're kind of a heavy guy, Lucca!"

He ran as fast as he could only to throw me abruptly into the water. As I unintentionally dove into the lukewarm waters, I could feel the ocean rocking me back and forth like a baby. It felt like a struggle to emerge to the surface, but it certainly was a welcomed shock. When I finally reached the surface to grasp for some air, I cleaned up my eyes and turned to Iris, who was laughing hard. I looked at Kevin, and he couldn't care less about my reaction to his spontaneous decision. Instead, he was wafting away like driftwood, eyes closed, moving back and forth with the tide.

I got out for a second to take off my soaking shirt since it was posing a heavy weight now that it was wet. Iris looked at me and took her beach dress off, revealing her unpretentiously good body in her red swimsuit. She ran to the sea and splashed in, later diving her head. She made me smile just by her pure enjoyment.

We stayed inside for a good hour goofing around. We talked about the tin box and its mysterious clues to a past life. We hypothesized about the different things it carried and the coincidence of finding such items after an accident. Life was good. That moment in time was a vivid reminder that life was easy and unpretentious. Life's simplicity was at its best, and it was gentle and kind to me. Maybe life wasn't a jerk. Maybe people made life into a problematic entity, with their ever adding impracticalities and tasks. Life should be simple and cheerful and worth living. We weren't spending a dime in having the time of our lives. We didn't have to work hard to reach this utopian state.

The sun became a palette of yellows, pinks, and purples. The sky was telling us it was about to start its unforgettable show. Iris decided to get out of the water, walking away from us. I looked at her and realized her beauty; the sun, shining on her body while she inconspicuously dried her damp hair. It wasn't about how vainly wonderful she looked in a swimsuit or how her eyes turned a hazelnut color as the sun shined on her face. She was a beautiful person, full of compassion and intelligence. She was the epitome of beauty—body, mind, and spirit. Like a Greek deity or an art nouveau goddess, she embodied everything good and beautiful in life.

As I reflected on Iris, I was staring at her like a maniac without noticing. She felt my eyes and looked back, catching me by surprise. Something else also caught me by surprise. A massive wave heading my way hit me and tumbled me until I ended up with my undergarments as full of sand as my burning nose. Her trance cost me my dignity, but it also turned my awkward staring gesture into an enormous laugh. I never understood how us men try to be so strong and perfect, and all it takes for a girl to notice you is life tripping you on purpose. I tried to clean myself up as much as I could and proceeded to walk as if nothing happened.

"Are you good? Was the sand tasty?" she sarcastically commented, all worth it just to see her smile.

"I'm good, a little salty and with a hurt ego, but everything else is ok," I replied while getting up from the wallowing experience.

"Here, have my towel, since I don't see you carrying one yourself." She wrapped the towel around me, which brought us incredibly close to each other. She giggled and turned away; maybe I was still looking at her like an idiot. She then looked down.

"May I have a bite of those lips?" she asked, looking back at me. She was still holding her towel with both hands, one on each side of the towel, trapping me in the best ambush of my life.

"Only if you want to," I replied. After all, I wanted to make sure my mind wasn't fantasizing about a situation and might be misunderstanding it due to hormones.

And so we kissed. While the sun was setting, like a cliche movie scene with background violins and camera close up. Except the mosquitoes were at it again, and my privates were itchy from the sand. But, hey! It didn't matter; life was perfect. I welcomed everything, even the soreness of a mosquito bite.

After a few seconds, we felt another set of eyes in our romantic encounter. Kevin was right in front of us, arms crossed, looking at us as the featured exhibit from a zoo. We looked at him and felt a bit embarrassed for our public display of affection. We stared down and kept busy for the sake of our pride. Kevin laughed at the scene and grabbed his phone, which was inside his flip-flops. He then took a picture of us and laughed again.

"Oh, come on, Kevin!" I complained. I was already used to his unapologetic humor; nevertheless, Iris was involved, so I thought I should look like I was doing something about it. Iris didn't mind a bit. She felt somewhat embarrassed, but she immediately grabbed her phone and set herself to take pictures of him.

The sun displayed a spectacular array of colors that increased in intensity as the nature behind us turned black. It was an outrageous scene that brought to life even the most secret feelings of awe. The colors were so vivid that they could turn even the most skeptic individuals into emotional beings. The birds slowly quieted, giving the crickets and cicadas a chance to add unforgettable sounds to an outstanding evening. There's no place on earth where colors are so intense, where life is so well lived. It filled my heart with joy and emptied my troubles into the ocean. It became an almost religious experience.

CHAPTER VIII

I must be looking for something

The morning after our perfect evening, I woke up completely renewed. I secretly smiled, thinking of every memory that came to my mind regarding Iris. That day I remained at the house, equipping it for my stay. I purchased adequate supplies and organized my old room to accommodate my needs. Kevin was visiting for a week or so, according to his wife's angry words over the phone. He seemed immune to her rage, though, like a professional shrink. He surely had patience over other people's behavior. I felt a divine providence in his stay; we were polar opposites, and he was five years my senior, yet I was learning immensely from him. I learned how not to take everything so seriously, how laughter was the best medicine, and how work was meant to afford joy instead of living to work, like in New York. He appeared to be contemptuous with life and in a permanent joyous state.

"Is she still mad at you?" I asked Kevin, just making sure he wasn't covering his emotions with fake positivity.

"Well, Lucca, when you get married, you figure out that it is better to give each other some space once in a while, to release tensions and miss each other enough to find forgiveness."

"Can you print that as a bumper sticker?" I jokingly suggested. To tell you the truth I was quite impressed with his deep thought. I knew who to call now when my woman turned into an enigma. He smacked me in the head and smiled, offering me eggs for breakfast.

As we sat at Mom's table, Kevin told me he was looking into the tin box pieces online to see if he could find any clues.

"I looked up the last name in the card, and there's nothing about a particular person," he said while stuffed with scramble eggs. I was kind of disappointed; I wanted to hear some new information on the subject. The eggs were good though, so I didn't complain out loud.

"I did find a place, Prussia, but it doesn't exist anymore."

"Well, that's a start... Wasn't that a kingdom

Germany took over?" My high school years appeared to be finally useful.

"Yes! According to Wikipedia, 'Prussia was a historically prominent German state that originated in 1545...' blah, blah, blah... 'House of Hohenzollern'... Nazi regime... Look! The picture is exactly like the insignia from the necklace!" He handed me the phone to show me the black eagle from the pictures.

"Kind of creepy. Why would Mom have some Nazi memento hidden in her wall?" I said, already surprised by the veracity of the items inside the box.

I kept scrolling down, and I saw many pictures of different people from the Prussian kingdom. I drew closer to see them and noticed many of them had a "necklace" similar or identical to the one I found inside the tin box.

"Wait a minute! This is no necklace, Kevin; this is a medal!" I abruptly interrupted Kevin while grabbing the heavy collar.

"She probably thought the medal was worth the money and stored it inside the wall or something." As absolute as I tried to make myself sound, I wasn't sure why my mom would be even remotely interested in German souvenirs.

"Besides, this medal is from a kingdom much older than Nazi Germany, so it might just be a coincidence," Kevin added, recovering from the shock of the new development.

While we were checking up the livery collar—apparently that's the name of those medals —my phone rang.

"Hello?"

"Hey, neighbor! It's Iris. How are you?" I was exceedingly happy about the call.

"Iris! How are you? Wait, how did you find my number?" It was foolish of me to ask, but I did anyway out of curiosity.

"Don't flatter yourself, Lucca, although I really wanted to hear from you, I'm calling from the hospital to give you news about your mother."

My body froze, and the blood drained from my face. I didn't want to hear the possible information of a worse diagnosis or, even more terrible, a death.

"Don't worry, it's good news," she added, almost reading my mind.

"Your mom showed signs of consciousness early this morning, and just now, she slurred a name:

Luis." Luis was my father's name and her husband of 30 years.

"That is great news! Can I go see her?" I was so excited to hear her voice again. Mom's, I mean. Not that it wasn't a perk to listen to Iris's voice, I could go as far as to say that the only thing that seemed to take her off my mind was the little tin box.

So, I informed Kevin of the splendid development. He was relieved, in part because he adored my mom's free spirit and independence. He grew up in a house with very structured environment to the point of asphyxia so he used to visit Mom whenever he felt choked by his father's demands and his mother's obliviousness. Mom was a safe haven for him. She was family, so he was allowed, and Mom's house was far enough to avoid a sudden inspection from his parents. He didn't do a thing to prove his parents right; he mostly hurt himself unintentionally by playing around the farm or surfing in the ocean.

Kevin saw my guard finally come down after all the stress I went through.

"If you want to go visit her, you can use my car. I want to go see a friend that used to surf with me a while back if you don't mind," replied Kevin.

"Sure, that would work out just fine!"

I was excited. Excited about the good news. Excited about the new relationships. Excited about the new secrets coming to light. So I got ready, hat included, and headed to the car. I noticed life was being gentle with me. We were friends again. We were at peace and ready to be with each other. I felt that life's unexpected situations weren't so impossible and detrimental to my future. It's funny how the same problem can mean the world to a person, or it could just be a tiny dent in a used car, you know, like the ones you hardly see and don't mind at all.

So I drove to the hospital as cautious as I could, keeping in mind that it had been a long time since I last steered the car on such sinuous roads. They are deceitful indeed; they charm you with their beauty only to show you that a vehicle is coming undoubtedly close to you and at a menacing speed. Sometimes it's too late to react to such situation, as my mom experienced. Upon arrival I called Iris to the number she previously called me from, only to figure out I landed at the hospital's mainline. So, I got out of the car and slammed the door as if the vehicle conspired against me to avoid a romantic encounter. I realized I still carried the tiny key from the tin box by the sudden movement. I put my hand inside my pocket just to feel it was safe. As I walked to the hospital's entrance, I fixed my hat and my shirt to look presentable.

By then, I already had paperwork stating I was on the waiting list to get an admissions card (I was sure I wouldn't have an admissions card in the near future, since inefficiency doesn't allow for such things to happen). As I arrived, I greeted the security guard at the front door and headed to the same hospital wing as before. Entering the hospital wing, I saw some previously occupied beds now available. These empty spaces were whispering in my ear, reminding me that any condition that seemed present could also be momentary. Each available bed, all dressed up for a future patient, was a somber symbol of the only two available options to leave the hospital: either recovered or dead. I headed to Mom's bed, number 112. I saw what could only be described as life back into her body: a better color in her skin, steadier breathing, and a more composed body position.

I grabbed her hand as I procured an unannounced sigh. It was moving to see Mom come back into the land of the living. I saw the possibility of hearing her voice again in the future. I imagined her back to dancing her Zumba lessons, or her beach drives on her Vespa. I could see it now. I felt she coul hear me, so I talked to her. I explained to her about the trip, the house, and the door... until we reached the tin box. Right when I explained my discovery, she moved, squished my hand, and slurred an unfamiliar name: Alfredo. She appeared to be holding on tight to that hope, apparent by the squeeze she gave my fingers. This information mattered to her. It was so significant in her life that she collected all her strength from her weak body and used it to communicate a name that didn't mean anything to me. It was both surprising and insightful. It gave me a sense of duty to find out what those random items were.

"Hello there, Lucca," Iris suddenly said in a low but distant voice.

"Hey, Iris, how are you?" I decided to greet her in the very Costa Rican kiss on the cheek, pending her approval as I got closer.

She looked at me surprised and smirked, as she replied:

"More importantly, how's Aura?" Iris already memorized my mother's name from the medical chart. She arrived to take her vitals and to check for abnormalities.

I looked at her with a sense of respect and wonder, for I could see a very tenacious woman that decided to become fragile in my presence the other evening. I felt humbled by knowing this. She took some notes after checking Mom up.

"Aura is doing a lot better today than the last time you came," she reassured me with a smile.

"I'll suggest for her transfer from the ICU to another wing," Iris concluded from the vitals.

"Really, that's amazing! I hope everything progresses appropriately!" I was still worried about her fragile state. After all, they weren't sending her home.

Amid the positive news, I asked Iris when she would clock out.

"I just have to take the vitals of eight more people, and I'll be out for the afternoon," she replied.

"I can wait for you at the *Soda* around the corner," I suggested to her. After all, I wanted to get to know Iris more. I had to understand she was in high demand, and she should focus on the people inside the hospital. The *Sodas* in Costa Rica are little cafes that offer various food, particularly during lunchtime, when they sell their famous *"Casado"*. *"Casados"* are the typical Costa Rican lunch plate. It consists of white rice, beans, plantain, salad, and a choice of meat. I was already hungry, in need of lunch, so the situation was favorable.

"That sounds interesting…" she replied while putting her hands on her chin and moving her fingers up and down, just like a piano player on a crescendo progression.

"Sounds like a plan," she finally decided.

I walked to the *Soda* after kissing my mother goodbye, anxiously waiting for Iris to be available. The place was quite irregular; a clandestine garage converted into seating for hungry customers. The food smelled delicious, so I sat at a table right at the corner of the space. A young waitress, maybe in her mid-20s, came to attend the table. I ordered soursop juice with a *Casado*. The sea breeze was blowing gently enough to be pleasant, and the weather had already cooled down a few degrees from the earlier midday sun. Ater calling Renzo back to inform him of Mom's favorable news, I decided to do a little research myself on the tin box items while waiting for Iris. I already knew the livery collar belonged to a Prussian character. I also knew that the last name of the person who used to own the old admission card was the name of an area instead of a regular surname. I couldn't comprehend why Mom would consider the name Alfredo so relevant after telling her the tin box's story. So I merged the two just to see if I could find more information online.

"Alfredo de Prusia," I mumbled to myself, as I always do when performing a task.

Suddenly, a list of articles and information appeared on the screen of my mobile device.

Alfredo of Prusia. He existed; there were pictures of him and information. As I read, I noticed that he was considered the last Prince of Prussia and lived most of his life in Costa Rica. This information blew my mind. Monarchy in a small country such as Costa Rica. And more importantly, why would my mother hide items related to a deceased monarch inside a wall? Why did they emigrate to Costa Rica? So many unanswered questions. As I was digging deeper into an informational spiral, I felt a small tap on my shoulder. It was Iris, already arriving from the hospital. She sat next to me, crossing her legs and with her elbow on the table. Her back tilted a bit into my research, and her chin rested on her hand.

"What have you found so far?" It seemed I was becoming the source of entertainment for most of my acquaintances.

"While in the hospital, I was testing my mom's consciousness by telling her the story of the tin box."

"And did she show any signs or respond to your information?" Iris asked. For her, my mother's welfare was far more critical than any story or conversation we could possibly have. I appreciated that.

"She did! Not only did she show signs, but she also slurred a name."

Iris was astonished at my information. She couldn't believe a person with days of such a severe condition could verbally express a word. Iris immediately got her phone out of her fabric bag and dialed a contact. She spoke in very sloppy Spanish to a person from the hospital, telling them the news.

When she finished with the call, she looked at me, clueless about what the conversation was before, so I ignored the subject, then I asked her if she wanted to go somewhere else.

"Where?" she asked, looking at me like if I had some grandiose plan.

"Would you like to have some coffee at my house? I can show you what I have found so far regarding my bizarre tin box. We can also watch the sunset from the balcony."

She overthought the situation, and then she explained to me:

"Lucca, I like you very much, but I think we are going way too fast for my comfort."[J9]

I was so tone-deaf. I was by no means planning a naughty way to take her into my bed. Not to sound old fashion, but my mom didn't raise me that way, and I respected her too much to be that pretentious. I frowned, and my eyes popped out from the misleading invitation.

"Oh, no, no! I didn't mean it that way! I just pictured us having a quiet afternoon on the balcony! Nothing else!" By the time I finished my sentence, my hands were already up to my chest, frantically moving left and right.

Iris raised a brow and crossed her arms. It was intimidating to see her doubt my intentions, but then again, we didn't know each other enough to read our mannerisms or tone of voice. We just knew we liked each other.

"Ok, let's do that, but only if you can drop me off before 9 pm. I need to wake up early tomorrow to take care of your mama. Deal?" She extended her hand as a sign of good faith—very executive of her. I felt I was signing a contract more than having a date.

"Deal." I shook her hand and looked at her in the eyes. Her very dark pupils felt like a mysterious pool of deepness, ready to trance me into an eternal extasis. I could very well be at her mercy anyhow; it was no use to try and take charge.

So I paid for my lunch, and we headed to the car.

CHAPTER IX

Do you believe in Magic?

As we got inside the finca, I noticed the sense of wonder Iris had about the whole experience. The palm trees moved back and forth with every passing breeze. Iris's enthusiasm made her open the car window, which brought the guava trees' sweet scent right inside the car. The grass was in a remarkably green state, thanks to the local keeper, and the birds of paradise were in full bloom. The beach almond trees covered the entrance to the carport, making the parking area almost invisible to the wandering eye. An average arrival to my mother's house suddenly changed into a grateful experience, all because of Iris's reaction to the grounds.

"It's a picture perfect paradise!" she said after sighing. She was looking all around, touching every single flower that would be fortunate enough to visit the tips of her fingers.

"Why did you leave, Lucca?" Her inquisitive nature couldn't avoid asking the obvious question.

"Well, I was trying to make a better living, I guess." My answer was clearly not enough. She thought I was obviously in paradise. My chain of thought must have sounded ridiculous to her. At least that's what I read from her gasping.

"What else would be better than this?" she naively said. She didn't know that I agreed with her on the matter up to a point, but paradise is not only about the land that is inhabited, but also about the stability and resources that the population possesses to create peace of mind amongst its inhabitants.

I wasn't about to give her an economic breakdown of the country, though. Not that I didn't think she'd care, but given the circumstances I wouldn't consider it suitable for a first date. So I smiled and politely pointed at the entrance to the house, as if my whole hand was showcasing a precious artifact. The structure of the house is charming, so it was part of a very favorable landscape. I know, regardless of its beauty, that this paradise's appearance was superficial in nature. Life deceives us that way; we all think of the unknown as having less defects than what we currently experience. Think about it: we feel if we strive for the job or the relationship we don't have, that somehow our current situation will come to a solution. But that new job, even though it might come with less financial strain–hopefully that's the case–it could also come with new challenges and worries. Same on a relationship. I guess that's what they call contempt; the ability to find happiness in the present circumstances.

"This is so charming! Did you live here growing up?" Her deep black eyes still wandered back and forth, storing as much information as possible.

"Part of my life. Unfortunately education wasn't very strong around here when I was growing up, so we had to move to the city for a while, in order for me and my brother to attend a good school."

Not long after getting inside, her eyes gravitated towards the living room, where she set her gaze on the table.

"Is that the tin box you were talking about?!" She quickened her walk, heading straight to the box. Her hands were already extending on her way to the table, as a child about to be lifted up by her parent.

"Can I touch it?"

"Sure, go ahead, maybe you would have ideas on how to solve the mystery"

She grabbed the box like it was the most breakable object. Piece by piece she looked at the different items, asking for the information I had so far. She paid close attention and reserved her opinion, like a scientist about to establish a hypothesis. After most consideration and thought, she clapped her hands and rubbed them together, gesturing she now owned the dilemma.

"So, basically all we know is that these objects did belong to a person with connections to the Prussian aristocracy," she efficiently summarized. Then she grabbed the livery collar and lifted it up:

"Do you know if this medal belonged to this Alfred from Prussia?"

"No idea. All I know is that it is Prussian"

"What about the picture? By the looks of it, its ancient."

"Yes, but it has no name or date, so we wouldn't easily know if it's the same Alfred guy."

"What about the paperwork? Does it have some sort of number we can look for in the database in the hospital records? I can look that up." Iris had a marvelous idea with her access to the hospital's network that might prove to bare fruit.

"Take it with you," I told her, aiming for her to

want to see me again in the near future.

The tea kettle I started before discussing my findings was already singing its customary whistle, calling me to tend the stove.

"Do you want some coffee? I asked her, while lifting my finger and pointing at the kettle.

"Coffee? Isn't it a tea kettle?"

So I smiled because by then I knew how much Iris loved new experiences.

"Have you ever tried Costa Rican hand-brewed coffee?"

"What? I want some! What is it?" I felt like the smartest guy on the planet, especially after her face brightened at her coming venture.

Iris walked to the kitchen to see what I was doing. I grabbed my mom's pour-over coffee maker, which consisted of an old wood base with a hole, a wired fabric called "the sock" and a tin white cup. I got the coffee out of my mom's pantry and served a full tablespoon for every cup of coffee to be made. Then I grabbed the kettle and poured the hot water slowly onto the sock where the coffee was placed. The aroma of the coffee slowly conquered the air, invading our sense of smell. That's the way Costa Rica smells; inside every home it smells like freshly poured coffee, and outside like wet fruit and greenery.

"So, if you really want to be a tica, you would drink coffee with no milk nor sugar," I explained to her while handling a cup of coffee. No English cup of course. I meant a decent-sized, tin mug of coffee.

"I'm certainly not going to do that." She laughed, already in premonition of the bitter taste that might be left on her tongue after such bravery.

"For the rest of us mortals, there is milk and sugar," I explained as I passed the sugar and milk. No fancy containers, just a carton of milk and a clear glass jar as a sugar container.

We sat outside and talked about life, starting with my mom's medical details. Then she asked the million dollar question I knew was tickling her curiosity since she arrived at the house:

"How was it, growing up here?"

"We spent the weekdays in San José, on a rental property by the school. Fridays we religiously headed here, to meet friends and play at the beach," I replied, waiting for her to dig deeper, as she always did.

"Do you miss it?"

"Well, I came to understand that my experience

had a context that changed overtime," I stated like a formal introduction to a college colloquium.

"What do you mean, exactly?"

"Well, first, there is the childhood factor. As a minor, I had no clue of the struggles my mother was having at the time."

"Of course, children are oblivious to their family's misfortunes unless they are in precarious conditions," Iris replied.

"Exactly. Then there's also the country's context back in the day, which is different than now, even for a child."

"Meaning?"

"A child growing up in the 90s in Costa Rica hardly had technology of their own, neither did his friends. You add that boredom to a beach setting, and the combination becomes a memorable childhood," I explained to Iris.

"Even in the cities that was the case."

After my psychological theory on why my experience in present day Costa Rica cannot be based on my past, Iris asked me for the real reason why I moved to New York.

"You see, everything looks wonderful here in Costa

Rica, until your wage becomes a Costa Rican wage. Some people are lucky enough to afford a trip to the US and buy their yearly clothes and electronics, but after five years of using the same furniture and appliances, you start to borrow money to afford a newer possibility. These loans have exorbitant interest rates–up to 12%–which take a big chunk off your monthly income. If you try to make a living by having a small business, the taxes will soar the prices of your goods to the unaffordable category. The only way to afford paradise is not by being born in paradise, but by earning in a developed country. You can achieve this by either working remotely or retiring with a developed-country pension." Iris understood the reason for my departure. She didn't blame me. It was, after all, the only thing that might keep me in good economical standing.

Iris then explained to me her life passions and philosophy, and then asked me what I thought with much attention. She seemed to be the type of person that liked deep conversation and wasn't concerned with controversial topics; not because she liked controversy, but because she craved understanding and knowledge. We joked about anecdotes from New York and our respective childhoods as we watched the sunset. The purple and pink hues intoxicated our visual as everything around us became a surreal setting. The mountains framed the sunset far upon the ocean, lost in brown and orange tones. Everything was pleasant and effortless. We moved from the outdoor sitting area on the balcony to the hammock. We sat together, caressing each other. Her face, now on my lap, looked like a masterpiece. The curves of her cheeks evoked tenderness in my heart by just looking at them. She was holding a piece of her dress in her hands, a playful thread at the hem. Her eyelashes, the biggest, darkest lashes I had seen in my life, felt like an earthquake every time she closed her eyes. They were intimidating, an impenetrable secret that wasn't easy to uncover. So, the only thing left to do was to cover them, in hopes of a more valiant sensation to achieve a kiss. Her face, now backwards from the romantic exercise, saw my chin as a perfect dessert for such a feast. Slowly she grabbed my cheeks and moved my face to surrender to her fate. She kissed my chin and back to my lips, where she finished by looking at me in the eyes, already uncovered by my trembling hand.

"You're like a drug, Iris. The one kiss you give me keeps me in a trance all week, thinking about you." I expressed right there what I could say to the best of my ability. It was no Shakespeare sonnet or Neruda's poem, but I really felt that way. She laughed at my expression, then toyed with my hair and said:

"You also raise my happy chemicals to the roof,

Lucca." She understood my archaic explanation to the point. It was exciting to be understood so well.

Suddenly, a door banged harshly in the distance, almost like Kevin wanted the whole Quepos to know he arrived.

"Kevin, you're going to break another door!" I shouted at him because in all seriousness, I also wanted to avoid another door incident.

"Sorry, man! I had to let you know I was here! I don't want any surprises from you two!" As always, Kevin's honesty was proven to change my face's color to a sudden red. Maybe he enjoyed my embarrassment. I tried to throw my reaction under the rug, but the color was there, which made Iris laugh, and then kiss me on the forehead.

"You're cute, even when you feel embarrassed." At least I got something out of it. Suddenly I wanted to be embarrassed more often.

Kevin dropped the keys on the counter and came over outside, bringing a can of mosquito repellent to us.

"Hey, guys! How are you?" he casually asked while resting his hands on his hip.

Iris looked into my eyes and said:

"Remarkable." Then she smiled at Kevin and stood

from the hammock.

Kevin stared at me with his eyebrows raised up almost to his hairline, his eyes wide open. His chin was down his neck, suggesting an unbelievable affirmation. To change the subject, and the oddness of the situation, I deliberately got up and walked towards the living room to start a conversation on our new discoveries regarding my family's time capsule.

"Apparently, Kevin, the name we were looking for was Alfred of Prussia."

"How do you know?"

"Mom told me."

"What? She's speaking now?"

"Just a bit," added Iris.

"Have you figured something out about him?" asked Kevin, ready to do some serious investigation.

"Yes. He existed, and he lived here, in Costa Rica." I throughly explained the information I got from my quick wait at the *Soda*.

"He's a descendant of the Prussian dynasty; his mother and father fled sometime during the First World War. He seemed to be a Nazi antagonist, at least that's what the local newspaper said in an article written about his family a while back."

"Interesting..." Kevin was already trying to calculate the next step of our research.

"I'll look into the hospital records, to see if there's more information on Alfred," Iris spoke up, ready to be part of the team. It was quickly becoming an adventure.

Kevin walked to the living room and grabbed the picture.

"Is this Alfred?"

"He didn't look like the pictures online, and also it doesn't match his timeline." I was certain that picture belonged to a museum instead of a tin box.

"And there's also the key," I reminded everyone, while getting the key out of my pocket and up in the air

"Nothing on that either?" said Kevin.

"I've been trying it all over the house, but every keyhole I see is a newer, bigger version."

"That's because that's not a door key, silly!" said Iris. Of course it was obvious to her. I'd never had any sort of small storage, neither had Kevin.

Kevin and I were suddenly looking for small boxes all over the house, while Iris went slowly to grab her purse.

"Lucca, it's time to go, I have to be at the hospital in the morning,"

I stopped my historical quest and grabbed my wallet and the keys, showing them to Kevin, asking for permission to borrow his car again.

"Sure, go ahead," Kevin replied, while defeatingly seating on the couch, giving up on the jewelry box search.

CHAPTER X

Under pressure

I went to bed late that night. New thoughts of Iris, hypotheticals about my mother's condition, and the ifs of history's secrets didn't let me catch any sleep. I was woken by the sound of my cell phone, calling from the same number Iris called me from before, so I smiled, thinking she was already missing me.

"Iris, has it been too long?" I teased her, expecting a flirty laugh in response.

"Hola? Hello? Sir? I'm calling from the Max Teran hospital, you appear to be the new contact number of Aura Vega Labrador, is this correct?" The blood that so easily streamed through my whole body seconds before suddenly stopped as I felt the earth shift.

"Yes, my name is Lucca, I'm her son. Is she ok?"

"We're sorry to inform you that Aura had a fatal

aneurysm this morning. We're going to need you to come to the hospital's morgue to identify…" My ears started emitting an acute sound again, and my heart felt like it stopped, my nose couldn't grasp for air, and my hands were sweaty.

"What?!" I yelled, processing the information. I tried getting up from bed, only to succumb to the floor with blurry vision. In the background, I could hear an echo of a voice, while someone opened my bedroom door.

"Lucca?! Lucca?! Are you ok?!"

Everything turned black after that. My body couldn't take the news. Physiologically, I was incapable of processing my mother's death.

I woke surrounded by emergency medics in their traditional Costa Rican blue jumpsuits, who were trying to wake me from what I thought was a terrible nightmare. The minute I opened my eyes, I wanted to run and scream, but I couldn't. My body shut down when I needed it the most. Kevin approached me from the back of the crowd.

"Hey, Lucca! You scared me! What happened?"

As I tried to express what was already obvious in my head, I couldn't really find the words. I looked down as tears dropped from my eyes to the floor and took a deep breath.

"Mom is dead, Kevin. They called me from the hospital. I have to go and identify the body."

Kevin knew how close I was with my mom. He understood my reaction well enough to grab my phone and ask me for my passcode.

"1029," I instinctively told him. It made me cry even more. There was no coincidence to that password. My mom used that same password on her card, which she taught me since I was a teenager.

Kevin started by calling the hospital to confirm the event. He then called his contacts on funerary arrangements.

"Lucca, do you know if your mom had any particular plan in the event of her death? Any will or last wishes?" Kevin was already a veteran at this; he had to bury his dad not long ago. I wasn't home when my own dad died, so I was new to the logistics behind the death of a loved one.

"I don't know. All I know is that she kept all her paperwork in her file cabinet, right in her office," I explained to Kevin with a burdensome tone. I was trying to give him as much information as I could, but my brain wasn't working at all.

The paramedics explained to Kevin a few things before packing their gear and leaving. Kevin looked at me and talked to them. They looked at me and talked to Kevin. A dynamic that happened a few times before finally saying goodbye. By then, I was already sitting on the bed with the help of one of the medics, who also asked if I was feeling better. The Red Cross in Costa Rica is a very important organization. Most of the personnel are volunteers who also ask for donations once in a while. No one dares to say no to that noisy can with a Red Cross painted on it. As proven by many people like me right then, you never know when you're going to need them.

I could hear Kevin looking around the house for the file cabinet. I didn't feel like helping. I just felt an empty stomach and a desperate mind. I remembered a poem I found when I was browsing inside the library, explaining the feeling that comes when a parent dies:

"We say goodbye to that one man

That held the whole world on his shoulders

And we progress to become

the brand-new orphans and loners."

That was exactly how I felt; like a brand-new orphan. My mother was gone, and now the whole world would forever rest on my shoulders. I felt alone. My mother was my confidant, my advisor, and my support during harsh times. She was the one who didn't judge but cared. No one else in this world was as loving and caring. Then I remembered Renzo. How was I going to break the news to him? I could hardly express the situation myself, let alone explain it to someone else. But I had to do it. If it was the other way around, I would like to know as soon as possible. So I dialed his number, secretly wishing for him to already know. The phone rang one time… two times… three times.

"Hello?"

"Renzo, it's Lucca, how are you?" I was playing the same game he played with me when he broke the news of my mom's accident. I was deviating the conversation to give me time to think about the words I should choose to express such dismal. It wasn't working though.

"Lucca! I'm good! What's up?"

I took a deep breath. He noticed the pause, and worried as much as I once did.

"Renzo, I have bad news, are you sitting down?" I remembered what just happened to me, and was avoiding a situation like the one I just went through, especially because I could hear the city noise in the call. He was out, and in public.

"It's Mom, isn't it? She's probably not doing well, and you want me to…"

"Renzo, Mom died," I interrupted him. I couldn't take it any longer. There isn't a good way to say it.

There was a pause in the call. I could hear noise, but he was absent.

"Renzo, are you there? Did you hear what I said? Are you ok?" I desperately asked, thinking about scenarios in which he might need help, with no one around that cared.

"I'm here, I'm here." I could hear him sobbing on the other side of the line. I wanted to be there for him. He needed someone to help him go through this horrendous sorrow.

"God, it's so hard…but how? I thought she was doing better!" He cried, trying to make sense of all of this. I could hear a female voice near him asking if he was ok. He wasn't ok, and I just hoped for her to notice him enough to be there, just like Iris did for me when we met.

"Let me call you back, Lucca." He wasn't going to call me soon. He needed time to process his feelings, to go home, to figure out what to do.

I was still in shock myself, still trying to stay in my reality instead of my imagination. Suddenly the clocks around the house were noisy, and the dripping faucets were too much to bear, so I took my phone and went to the balcony, hoping to resurrect with the sounds of nature into a new, more resilient creature. As I headed outside, the phone rang. It was Iris. I didn't know how to react to her. I felt a certain irrational rage at the hospital's staff. It was too sudden, so I felt suspicious and hurt. I didn't want to try to be nice or gentle, I couldn't help it, so I didn't answer her call. I wished I had the strength to, but I simply couldn't deal with it.

"Lucca, here, try eating this." Kevin graciously brought me some canned soup, hoping I gained strength from it.

"Thanks, Kevin," I replied. It was as humbling as it could get. A person that you hardly visit, taking care of you like a child, while making arrangements to bury your mother. Under such a contract, I could see why people so easily forgive each other. When you feel this type of friendship, a selfless kind of compassion and understanding, you realize the meaning of brotherhood.

As I was sipping the warm soup, my senses weren't interested in its taste or smell. My palette was overwhelmed by the bitterness of my own tears. Suddenly, there was a knock at the door, uncharacteristic of an acreage in the middle of Quepos. Kevin rushed to the door, still finishing the last of his own soup.

"Hello, come on in," said Kevin, looking at me for a predisposed reaction.

From the door came in Iris, wearing her scrubs. She was coming straight from the hospital, secretly hoping for my heart to be in less pain than it actually was. It appeared she didn't mind about me not answering her phone call. I turned my head around, as if I didn't notice her coming into the house. My fingers were anxiously tapping the wood frame of the outdoor furniture. My body involuntarily was caring for something my mind tried not to care about. As she got inside, she looked directly at me, and then rushed to my side. I looked down, postponing a possible confrontation of my feelings, as if the floor would be able to erase my past if I just stared at it hard enough. I felt her small hand touching my fingers. Her skin was as cold as ice, probably from the rainy afternoon. She grabbed my chin with her right hand and lifted my head up. She was trying to get me out of my isolation into her world.

"Lucca, I'm so sorry about Aura." She moved on to touch my wavy hair, comforting me.

"I know I couldn't possibly understand what you're going through right now, but my heart feels heavy for your loss."

I took a deep breath, as if the air inside my lungs meant a brand-new take on life. I didn't feel like talking, so I still looked down, hoping everything would disappear. She looked at Kevin with a concerned face. Her eyes turned red as she squished her lips. Kevin simply shrugged as he couldn't figure out how to make me react to life.

"It's Okay, Lucca, I'm here for you, even if it means that you listen to me instead of the other way around."

She was persistently attacking my sadness. She was tackling it head on with her understanding. She wasn't letting go. She wasn't going anywhere.

"You said she was getting better. You gave me hope," I complained to her with a defeatist tone of voice.

She looked at Kevin, who looked at me in return as he stood still.

"Lucca, she's not to blame for what happened; she

tried her best," said Kevin.

"Were you there, Kevin? Making sure she got what she needed?" I unfairly reprimanded Kevin.

What he was saying was perfectly understandable, but that didn't mean I wasn't hurt.

"Lucca, I was there when she died," said Iris, trying to let me know what Kevin was saying was correct.

"Is that what you tell every single of your patients? Do they teach you that at nursing school and make you repeat it?" I was already enraged about life, and Iris was part of that hurricane.

"Thank you all for caring, but right now I just need to be left alone." I got up and left the couch.

I tramped to the bedroom and closed the door, in an effort to isolate myself once again. Sometimes people say irrational things to get away from a stressful situation, and this was clearly my attempt at it.

Kevin and Iris were hurt. They wanted the best for me, but I wasn't giving in or making it easier for them. I took my shoes off and went to bed. I wanted life to pass by quickly, as if my heart just needed time to be as it was before.

Sometime during that night people started

showing up with food. I knew that because I could hear the doorbell and people talking to Kevin for short periods of time. Eventually I could hear the mumbling, as if there were more people inside the home talking to one another, thronging in the social area of the house. Sometime late at night I heard less and less people, until I heard a last goodbye.

Kevin knocked at my bedroom door and opened it. He told me that he spoke to several people, including his mom, who was my mom's cousin; she gave him a detailed account of my mom's funeral arrangements. She wanted to be cremated; her ashes thrown to the sea. Kevin was explaining it to me as if I was replying anything to him. He knew it was too much to bear, so he left the room and made some calls. I couldn't even think about what Renzo was going through. He couldn't come here to visit, he couldn't see her one last time. He didn't have a Kevin who would be with him no matter what. He didn't have an Iris who would understand him forever.

Time passed by, me lying in bed. No hunger, no will to get up. Just hours and hours of intermittent sun and shade, and then night. Kevin would come in, drop food on my nightstand, talk to me as if I would help him figure things out, then go back out. Eventually, Kevin got inside my room one last time. He came in with a wooden box where my mother was laid to rest. Her ashes inside the box, her voice still inside my head. He also dropped some documents right next to her ashes. I assumed they were legal documents stating the cremation process, and put my phone right next to everything else.

"Lucca, here is everything you need on your mom's cremation," he said as he organized everything on the nightstand.

"I have to go to my family now, Lucca. My kids are already asking questions, and I miss my wife. I did everything I could to help you." He came closer to the bed as he spoke, finally sitting right by my side.

"Life isn't fair, Lucca, but it doesn't mean it isn't worth living." With those words he left. My eyes betrayed me; I couldn't lift my sight to say goodbye to him. My mouth couldn't express my emotions, or how thankful I was for him to be there. I heard the door close and the engine start. He was moving on, and I was stuck.

CHAPTER XI

*Life is bigger than you
and you are not me*

A couple of days went by. The phone kept ringing in vain, only to find an answering machine. Once in a while, Ed, the security guard, would pass by on his rounds to make sure I was still breathing. He would look through the window and stare at me for a couple of seconds. Then he would grab his phone from his pocket and make a call, maybe to Renzo, or perhaps to Kevin. I got up once in a while just to use the bathroom. I didn't shower or eat. My body ached from top to bottom. My head felt like I had a fever, but I wasn't hot at all. My stomach rumbled once in a while, only to find a careless mind and a broken heart.

On one occasion, I got up only to step on the key I'd been carrying around when I had adventures to think about. It hurt as much as when I was young and stepped on a misplaced lego piece.

"Ugh," I muffled while holding my foot.

My new foot pain woke my senses up; suddenly I was hungry enough to head for the kitchen. So, I picked up the key and put it in my pocket again, and headed out of my room for something to eat. If every mumble I heard in this house the night of the funeral brought a dish to share, I bet there was enough in the refrigerator to fill me up for at least a week.

I headed to the kitchen and saw the broken wall, a reminder of the accident that happened. Across the living room, the tin box containing my mom's mysterious riddles called upon my curiosity, even under sadness. I kept walking towards the kitchen and served myself a good portion of every single dish. I was starving, and the smell of those traditional dishes reminded me of my mother's cooking. I ate as much as I could: plantains in sugar cane syrup, gallo pinto, a bit of mondongo, and some palmito salad. Everything was delightful. While I was eating, the tin box kept calling me to share its secret, so I decided to eat on the coffee table instead of the kitchen. The phone rang again, but this time I felt emotionally available, so I picked it up.

"Lucca, thank God! I was so worried about you!" It was Iris, who apparently had called me at least ten other times.

"Iris, let me first say I'm sorry. I shouldn't have said what I said." There were a few seconds of silence. Almost as if she was waiting for the wound in her heart to be healed with more apologies.

"Iris, I don't think you are responsible for my mother's death," I emphasized, making it clear to her that my behavior was a cry from my soul not to go through such agony.

"You have been nothing but caring and gentle with me, and I don't want you to hate me for what I said. I'm just a fool with a hurting heart."

"Stop," she said as if commanding my emotions.

"It's ok if you're hurting, but it's not ok to make others hurt because of it."

"So this afternoon, after work, I'll go to your house. You can apologize to me in person. Right now, I'm going to call Kevin, because everyone is concerned about your well-being, even though you feel like the loneliest person in the world."

I had never heard that tone of voice from Iris. I guess I deserved it; after all, I did get mad at her for something completely unjustifiable.

"Fair enough. . . I guess it's the least I can do."

After our chat, she hung up, leaving me with

much to think about.

I decided to take a bath right away since it was highly probable I would see Iris that day. Not only that, but Costa Rican houses usually have no air conditioning systems in them, mainly because the cost of electricity is too significant to bear, which makes humidity a cause for stench on anyone. Locals know it; some even take a bath twice a day.

Sice there weren't any clean towels, I headed to the guestroom closet looking for more. The tall closet needed a ladder just to be able to access the top shelves were the towels where: right next to the bedsheets, where mom always placed them. I climbed the ladder to reach out to where the bed sheets were. I was able to see some old beach towels behind the bed sheets, so I got the bed sheets out and tossed them on the bed to finally reach them. As I reached for the towels, I saw a big cardboard box with my name on it. I was already feeling sentimental, so I also grabbed the old cardboard box, thinking it would contain my childhood mementos.

My hands were full of dust from the old cardboard box, so I clapped a few times before opening it. *"Lucca"* the box read, in my mother's handwriting, a fading memory itself. I pulled the old masking tape off, careful not to rip apart the box where Mom stored my old toys.

The box was full of clothes and drawings from my childhood. I took them out and stared at them, slowly tinkering each item while I tried to remember when such an occasion took place. I recognized one of the drawings, a family portrait, drawn in second grade, according to my own handwriting at the corner of the art piece. It was a very basic portrait of stick figures, giant faces, and a typical landscape behind us all. It was only me and my parents, since Renzo wasn't born yet. I kept digging in to see more items: a baby outfit, some old formal shoes meant for a toddler, a wooden train set that I used to carry around all over the house... So many little details my mom kept as a reminder of who I was as a child. You could see it all and determine what kind of child I was; restless child with lots of imagination–but zero artistic skills, apparently.

I was almost done with the cardboard box, every item out, with the exception of some wood box, all stained from food and with circular marks, probably from an old drink insistently settled on top of it. Dust covered whatever beauty was left behind. It was a dark mahogany jewelry box, heavy due to its metal incrustations and keyhole. As disgusting as it looked I took it out to see what was probably my own legal paperwork from my birth.

This woman loves boxes, I thought to myself. After

all, I kept finding her valuable souvenirs inside a box every time there was an item relevant enough to be kept safe. The box was understandably locked. Its small keyhole reminded me of the old key I had in my pocket, always with me since its discovery. I decided to give it a try, see if it could open the box. Sure enough, the tin box, with its rusted hinges, opened to the sound of an old trinket.

Aha! A birth certificate! I told myself with a good measure of nostalgia. Little did I know that it was exactly what I thought it was, but with very different information than what I imagined. The birth certificate had my name, my birthdate, but my last name wasn't my actual legal name. Not only that, but my father's name was also incorrect, or so I thought.

"Who is this?" I said to myself, thinking that maybe my mother kept someone else's birth certificate. I didn't know anyone with my name growing up, so it was odd, to say the least.

The phone rang. It was Renzo, calling me for the millionth time, after receiving news that I was back answering the phone.

"Lucca, how are you? Why weren't you answering the phone?" Renzo complained.

"Hi, Renzo, I'm sorry, I was so depressed after

what happened..." I couldn't help but sigh after the thought of it all.

"The thing is, Lucca, I was also depressed," he said.

"I guess we both dealt with death in our own way," I explained, just to avoid pointing fingers or a bitter conversation.

"I guess so."

Renzo knew I shut down when I experience a severe event. Breakups, fights with him... every time, I would stop socializing and focus on myself.

"Are you ok? How bad are you from 1 to 10?" I asked Renzo, just to have a measure of how much he needed help.

"I'm better than yesterday, so I'm assuming I'll be better tomorrow."

"Wise words, Renzo."

We talked about our feelings and our current situation. He asked about the legal aspects and if I needed help. It was a brand-new relationship happening in front of my eyes. Suddenly my brother was present, open to dialogue, and emotionally available. We chatted for hours. I told Renzo about Iris and my stupid reaction to her help. I explained to him in detail the eventful tin box find, and how random every piece of information was. He didn't seem to give it much thought, until I sat back on the bed, on top of the folder by mistake, and decided to tell him about the odd birth certificate.

"... I found all these mementos inside a wooden box, drawings, outfits of mine when I was little, and now I'm holding this birth certificate with the name Lucca on it...."

"You found it! God, Lucca, I'm so sorry you figured it out during this time; it wasn't meant to be like this," said Renzo, relieved of some heavy burden still unknown to me.

I stopped. My brain started to finally function towards the proper conclusion.

"What do you mean? What should I have found under different circumstances?" I didn't want to say it. It was hard enough to lose a parent, let alone figure out I had been lied to my whole life.

"Wait, what is it that you thought it was?" Renzo asked with a defeatist tone, already understanding that he said more than I had figured out myself.

"No, Renzo, if you know something I don't, just be straight with me and tell me what it is." I confronted Renzo right away; after all, a new connection between us appeared to be spurring, and honesty is the healthiest way to start any relationship.

"Well, Lucca, I understand your confusion; after all, we look remarkably alike."

I couldn't act very scandalized. My mind already went through an extreme overload of feelings and information not long ago, so I was already in a "don't care" kind of mood. I guess I was out of adrenaline. I took a deep breath to get ready for another punch in the face from life."

"Let me get this straight… Dad wasn't my father?"

"He considered himself your dad in all aspects but biologically," said Renzo. It was a very smooth way of telling me my stepdad actually raised me.

"Did he know?" I asked, my eyebrows unintentionally frowning, reaching each other as to receive the news together.

"Yes, Mom was pregnant already when they met."

"So, this birth certificate has the correct name of my father?"

"I think so, Lucca. Mom said she was going to tell you herself every time you visited, but on every trip, you came back without a clue."

"But why does he have the last name as an old

country?"

"Because your ancestors RULED that country."

The overemphasized word that Renzo suggested carried with itself a magnitude of questions. Why didn't my mother tell me about it? What were the implications of this identity since everyone was so willing to keep it a secret? Do I have a family I don't know about?

"There's a reason why you were so easily given a green card. Mom wrote a letter that she sent to the Immigration Office explaining your status as royalty, Lucca."

I was feeling weak already, and my head was hurting from the overload of information. I thanked Renzo for his rundown and hung up the phone. I sat on the bed, looking at the wall for eternity. First came a wave of curiosity. Then a second wave of rage. Finally, a sense of gratitude toward a man that wasn't even my dad and still worked hard to give me everything he could. My mom was a different story. Her decision not to tell me balanced my feelings out between the nostalgic sentiment of mourning and her humanity. She gave it her all. I guess that means that sometimes it is better not to disclose information.

I went back to the living room to look at the tin box items; after all, I now had a completely different perspective surrounding this mysterious story. I looked at the information online again, taking notes, making sure I followed this man who was my biological father. I read about his titles, and his dad, who fled Prussia in part to avoid Nazi indoctrination that my father and his sister would have been subjected to. I read about his good nature, his late marriage, and how he lived a modest life by choice. I was secretly proud of the principled move to a far away country. My grandfather left a life of luxury behind to avoid what was so obviously immoral. Many people were confused back in the day. Most people were oblivious or negligent. But he left everything behind. My grandmother, with two small children, managed to also embark on such a tedious journey. During the worst part of the Great War, he even suffered persecution when Costa Rica established concentration camps for Nazis–ignorantly enough, many people with German ancestry ended up accused or enclosed in this jail.

While my hands held my head as if it would fall off due to the current information, I heard the phone ring again. This time, it was Iris telling me she was off her shift and on her way to the house. I rushed to the shower with one of the old beach towels I searched for in the guest room. I took a shower while thinking about the next steps towards solving so many dilemmas in my life. As I got ready, I figured it was probably a good idea to call Kevin and ask him, since he's my mother's family too. He might be able to give me some answers. So I dialed his number, with the hopes of closure, or at least direction on my next move.

CHAPTER XII

Do You Know The Way to San José?

Saturday came, and as planned, I got ready to have a weekend trip to San José. Iris was all in by our last conversation, although I didn't know if it was her curiosity to explore the capital city or her desire to help me find the missing pieces of my story. Maybe it was just the fact that we clearly felt affection for each other. Perhaps it was a combination of excuses.

I took with me the only pair of jeans I brought for the trip and my hoodie. San José's temperatures are very different than Quepos. San José has, in my opinion, better weather conditions than the coastal provinces of Costa Rica. Its higher altitude brings constant winds that dry up the air, making it less humid. It also lowers the temperatures, making the area around 75 degrees year-round, give or take. The west of San José has more planned urbanization, making it more appealing to the eye, hence the better-designed buildings and cleaner streets. Escazú is the crown jewel of the west, with the most investments and priciest housing.

A knock on the door told me how familiar Iris was with the property; Ed didn't even call me to ask for authorization. That was ok though; Ed was more family than staff, and he knew when someone wasn't welcome. Iris and I both agreed to rent a car the night before, a little Kia Soul to help us reach our destination. We loaded the car with our weekend luggage and some snacks for the trip. Iris was excited, and this helped me get my mind off things. Every time I fell into a hole of memories and uncertainties, Iris was there to offer a free joke or gesture that would take my mind off bitterness.

We headed to San José, which meant to drive first through downtown Quepos. One can hear the ocean waves by just opening the window. The seagulls and pelicans were part of the visual landscape. *The Malecón*, a sidewalk stretch in downtown Quepos, was filled with pedestrians rushing to schools and businesses alike. Children were dressed in their customary blue bottom and white top school uniform: a traditional scene that served as a resting station for my turbulent family affairs.

On our way out of Quepos, vast palm plantations break into clearings that show historic wood houses. These houses were built when the area was first developed for international crop commerce. The wooden houses are mostly turquoise, built on a raised foundation. This architecture allowed the rainy season showers to flood the area without consequence. Earthquakes were also less traumatic for these houses since they were made of a more flexible material than its brick and mortar counterparts. Nowadays, you can see the space under the house used as a garage or with a couple of hammocks.

Iris and I enjoyed the scenery with music from her favorite playlist. Her lips were constantly singing the songs but also secretly calling me to their aid. Her white skin contrasted with absolute power the black tone of her hair. She told me stories in between songs about how she decided to become a nurse and how her parents met. She described to me her hometown of Scranton, Pennsylvania, and how her once humble, coal-mining family was able to go to school and make a living in the medical field. The conversation and the company made the trip a lot faster.

We stopped at a fruit stand to purchase mangoes in lime juice, *cajetas*, fried plantain, and candied fruit. *Cajetas* are a combination of sugar cane and milk or coconut. Iris thought the coconut cajetas were delicious, but the mango in lime juice proved to be her favorite snack. The acidity of the lime combined with the texture of the mango species that grow in Costa Rica makes it a memorable food choice. Even pregnant women crave this delicacy, as my mother used to remind me.

Back on the road, I hit the pedal at Route 27, the highway stretch that would take us straight to Escazú. It wasn't as busy as I expected. Going the opposite direction, however, would have required patience. The closer we got to Escazú, the more cars we saw driving in the opposite direction. Once we got to La Guacima, we ran into heavy traffic on our side as well. The trip wasn't enjoyable anymore; it became a war between drivers, each trying to advance faster than the car next to them. It was both stressful and ridiculous. People were honking, keeping themselves unsafely close to the vehicle in front of them, all in the hopes of avoiding another driver to take their space. I couldn't blame them. The eight-lane highway became a four-lane street after the tolls, creating chaos. After hours of traffic, we finally arrived at Escazú; a city with a good amount of interesting buildings and beautiful landscape. Tita, Kevin's mother, graciously let us stay in her home during our quest in San José, which was a great way to talk to her in between her naps and to save ourselves some money.

Her home is in a good-sized piece of

land up the mountain from downtown Escazú, in San Antonio, almost to reach the mountain peak. A well-maintained garden full of ferns and hydrangeas overpowers the view. The house is small by American standards, except for us living in Brooklyn. A 1940's Costa Rican style white bungalow welcomed us into its alcoves full of framed family pictures and vinyl furnishings. Her tiny figure, sitting in an upholstered chair looking at the front door, smiled at us. She reminded me so much of mom: her smile, her little wrinkles on the side of her eyes, her gestures. Maybe I was missing her too much, or maybe she did look like her cousin. Out came Kevin, who decided to meet us there.

"Lucca! How was the trip?!" He was genuinely happy to see me. He shook my hand and hugged me to follow up on his affectionate salutation.

"A little tired; traffic was terrible!" I complained as if he could do something about it.

Iris also gave Kevin a hug and immediately knelt on one knee to say hi to Tita.

"Hola!" said Iris with a thick accent. She was trying hard to relate to Tita, and she noticed her effort right away, so she extended her arms and hugged her as if she was a long-lost child who just came home.

You could tell Iris loved the welcoming aspect of the Costa Rican culture. Contrary to its American counterparts, Ticos believe strangers to be good people unless proven otherwise. On the other hand, Americans believe strangers to be undeserving of trust unless proven to be good people. It's a courageous way to socialize if you think about it. It also helps that Costa Rica is a small country, so gossip spreads fast if someone failed to keep a good standard of social interaction.

"Lucca, are you hungry? I cooked some Gallo Pinto for you guys."

I looked at Kevin as a hungry lion who just skipped a meal, never mind the tons of snacks we ate on the way to Tita's house. Kevin's Gallo Pinto is famous for its delicious taste. You could smell his cuisine a mile away.

"No way! Really? Kevin, you warm my heart," I teased. By now, I was used to his love language, which could easily be described as sarcastic humor instead of words of affirmation.

Iris came close to us while helping Tita. We were already moving towards the kitchen. I reached the pan full of Gallo Pinto to give it a try before serving. Suddenly I felt a substantial hit on my hand with a wooden spoon, enough to stop me from trying.

"No!" said Tita with a mom-type of reprimand.

"You have to wait, Lucca; Tita has to serve us," said Kevin with a quirky smile. He then explained the family dynamic:

"Every member of this family has a task we all depend on. Tita's task is to serve the food and fold the laundry."

It might appear a little archaic to some people, but everyone needs to have a purpose in their life. As we get older, maybe we can't take care of children or work, but we need a task to feel relevant. Seniors are usually disposed off in other cultures, but in Costa Rica, they stay home and help, which gives them purpose. Having a goal is a big part of happiness; without it, we feel unnecessary. When we feel disposable in a society, we become lonely and depressed. Iris understood this concept well, so much so that she lives her life helping other people.

"Well said, Kevin!" replied Iris while clapping to encourage more words out of his previous statement.

We sat down on the small dining table by the kitchen area, and Tita served us a plate of Gallo Pinto. Very slowly and steady, as a child who is just learning how to act. Kevin and Iris waited patiently. I wasn't so patient. Tita noticed and served me last to give me a lesson on the importance of serenity.

The Gallo Pinto was delicious. Its flavor is a combination of fried onions, bell pepper, and garlic, all mixed with rice and beans. Kevin adds Lizano sauce to it, which is imperative in many of the Costa Rican traditional dishes. He garnished the Gallo Pinto with cilantro, giving it a fresh flavor. Kevin keeps his share of secret spices all to himself, although I could probably bet he used cumin and chicken bouillon in the mix. He served it with canned tuna and salad. Costa Rican tuna is not just any kind of tuna. Costa Rican tuna is so good that Ticos living abroad fill their luggage with its cans to bring into the US this delicacy.

We all enjoyed each other's company for a while until, eventually, the conversation got serious enough to ask about my mom's past.

"Tita, do you know anything about my biological father?" I asked, hoping to get a good story out of her.

Tita smiled and looked up to the ceiling, almost as calling youth with her eyes. She put her hands together, getting ready for an almost soap opera finale of a story.

"Yes, Aura and the prince. Good old times when we

were young and in love!"

I smiled and waited for the continuation of what Tita introduced as an epic love story.

"Your mother was younger than he was but love has no age. Alfred was his name."

She told us how my biological father wasn't a pretentious person at all; to the contrary, he made an effort not to look the part, so much so that he was always humbly dressed, many times dirty with mud from his job or his land. He had an ordinary job back in the day as one of Cachi's hydroelectric power plant managers. There he met my mom, where she was an executive assistant. My dad was easy on the eyes and gentle with her. She was exciting and fearless. They complemented each other very well, to the point where they did everything together, even though it was only a six-month rendevous. They secretly fell in love. As curious as she was, my mother didn't understand why the relationship had to be secret. Eventually, she became pregnant. She happily brought the news to her love, only to discover the truth about his identity: he was a prince, and as such, he had responsibilities beyond his control when it came to marriage and family. He suffered as much as she did, so they decided to separate from each other. My mom took it literally; she went away to live her life in Quepos. She eventually recovered and fell in love with Renzo's dad, who took me in as his own son.

"What happened to Alfred? Did he stay in Costa Rica after that?"

"He lived and died here, in San Jose. He was buried in a cemetery in Purral."

"There was some sort of arrangement that you should be aware of, if I'm not mistaken."

"What is it?" said Kevin, sipping a boxed juice as he asked.

"I don't remember Aura telling me about it. I just know there is something amiss." Kevin looked at his mom as a terrible storyteller.

"Mom!" Kevin replied as if he turned into a child, nagging his mom about the story's outcome. Iris was already ahead of the game, thinking about the next move in our quest.

"We should go visit his tomb. It might give you closure," Iris suggested. I appreciated her psychological approach.

"Well, it's an intriguing story; thanks for sharing it with us." Tita probably enjoyed the visit as well as the gossip; nevertheless, we were intruding in her personal life by staying, let alone the remembrance of memories that might be painful.

The new information gave me so many other questions: who was the man in the picture? What were the consequences of the latest news I gathered? Should I try to keep in touch with my German relatives? There was someone alive out there in the world that was my relative for sure, maybe as lost as I was. Perhaps they had all the answers. Maybe there was a reason why my mother decided not to keep in touch. One thing was for sure: the quest for my past was helping me overcome the loss of my mother. I discovered information about her I never thought possible. In retrospect, this story helped my mother's memory become part of history instead of a loss in the here and now.

CHAPTER XIII

*Would you know my name
if I saw you in heaven?*

Off we went to bed, Kevin was sleeping in his room, Iris was in the guest room, and I was on the couch–I'm a gentleman, what can I say. I couldn't sleep that night. A combination of excitement and worry kept my eyes open. Iris wasn't sleeping at all either, and knowing that wasn't helping. She got out of the room to grab something to eat, stealthy, as if this were in one of her hospital wings. I looked at her for a while, avoiding being noticed, just observing how her dark, long hair reflected the night lamp light. Even in the shadows she looked exquisite, a charming spell of the best kind of magic. She noticed someone looking at her from behind, so she turned around swiftly, catching my naughty eye in the act.

"Can I help you?" she replied to my insubordinate eyes, while grinning at me.

I smiled and looked at her even more, as a child who just got permission to eat his favorite candy from the pantry. She grabbed some water and came closer to me, so I sat down, expecting her company.

"Not sleeping, huh?" Iris asked.

"Nope, I just don't know what the next step would be," I told her, concerned about the reason for my trip to San José. Iris always had the same effect on me when we talked; she made me forget my troubles to the point of disregard. Sometimes intentionally, as she supported me through this trial. Other times by just swinging around to say hi and ask me about life.

She looked at me and kissed me on the lips as if it was the most normal action between us. There was no oddness or misunderstanding. No anxiety about the expectancy of the moment. It was a couple-kiss. A regular romantic kiss that would add up to a lot more kisses and affections over time.

"Thanks for that, may I have more?" I dared to ask.

"More kisses?"

"More of you, whatever that might be." She smiled as I grabbed her back and moved her closer to my body, already steaming up for what might be next.

"Chiquillos terribles!" said an unsuspecting voice from the hall.

It was Tita, moving along one step at a time as she tried to reach the sought after destination of the living room. We composed ourselves from the moment, fixing ourselves to look obedient in front of her.

"What is keeping you up, apart from the fact that you don't want to be apart from each other?" She was as honest and open as Kevin. I couldn't even imagine an argument between those two.

"We were discussing what to do next," I explained to her, as if Iris and I were sitting down strategizing for hours.

"What did Max say?"

"Wait, who's Max?" asked Iris.

"Max?!"

"Max, your mom's lawyer, she should know about the situation. She probably has her will."

"God, how could I forget? She's probably expecting my call!"

I got the phone from the living room table, and looked for lost calls. There it was. Max called me twice when I decided not to answer the phone. She was aware of my mom's passing and tried to help me through the legal aspect of it. I was too depressed for my own good and didn't take the call. It was late at night, so I settled my urge for answers until Monday, when Max would be at the office for sure.

"You can visit Alfredo's grave, or trace his steps to the so-called Cachí area, as Iris suggested," Tita cleverly reminded me with a wink.

"I guess we can do that. We can head to the tomb tomorrow, maybe have breakfast close by, then head to Cartago and check out Cachí." I organized the trip's logistics to make sense.

"Sounds like a plan, let's go to bed then," Tita said. She was politely pushing us away from a romantic encounter, probably traumatized by Mom's unplanned pregnancy.

We all decided to go to bed for the sake of our new adventure. Having a plan helped me put my thoughts together. Now I was able to close my eyes and feel tired.

Next morning we headed to Purral, Guadalupe. We were excited and hopeful for the trip. It was a sunny day in my mind, although I was still a bit confused about my roots. The clouds in the sky didn't seem to follow me around, as they usually did. We left at 9 a.m., and had a less eventful ride than the traffic packed arrival to San José. Iris was secretly amused at the whole "searching for a prince's background" situation. I couldn't blame her, it was a story worthy of a Hallmark movie, even with its turbulent deaths and accidents. Hopefully it wasn't going to become a Halo apocalyptic scene anytime soon.

The trip looked promising, an interesting combination of discovery and history. As we moved through the famous rotondas and bridges, characteristic of Costa Rica's capital city–and a Russian roulette of traffic, if you ask me–Iris discovered the real Costa Rican life: a mess of cars and lack of economic means, meshed together to form a fallen paradise. What was once fertile soil and beautiful views was now a cluster of concrete and vehicles, all making the sounds of a city too poor to prosper yet too beautiful to leave behind. The more we drove into the city, the more tragic the scene became. Once we reached Purral, it already became an appalling view: *"tugurios"*, houses made up of old zinc roof sheets and trash, behind the main street. Poverty was now more visible than ever. The face of Costa Rica no one advertises, the one no one wants to see. The part of Costa Rica that is in dire need to be noticed due to its lack of resources.

"This is terrible? Do people here have basic needs?"

Iris asked, already feeling the lack of all these people as a burden in her heart.

"They have water and electricity, and for sure cable, probably at least one cell phone in the family," answered Kevin from behind. Kevin decided to join us last minute, just to make sure we didn't get lost or in trouble.

"Costa Rica is one of the few countries in Central America with drinkable water throughout the country. Electricity is also considered a human right. Cable, not so much, but hey, one can be unemployed, but not bored, right?" I joked out loud to ease the shocking view.

"Remember when I told you to be careful with gangs and violence in the city?" said Kevin again, trying to make a lesson of it.

"Well, this is it. This is the place where you watch your back and avoid visiting after hours."

It had been a long time since the last time I felt that unsafe. When growing up in Costa Rica, we hardly visited the east side of the country, let alone the inner neighborhoods. My old school was in Escazú, and my parents usually let me stay at home when they needed to run errands in such places.

"Is it as bad as it looks?" Iris asked.

"That depends on your definition of bad. It isn't as bad as most countries in Central America, hence the amount of Nicaraguans living under such conditions." Kevin was explaining the harsh reality to Iris: Nicaraguan immigrants rather live under these precarious conditions than go back to their home country. In Costa Rica they have basic needs such as health care and education for their kids, also the needs previously listed by Kevin. Still, work was irregular and as a consequence money was a frustrating topic in such households.

It's not all positivism when addressing such benefits. To achieve such privilege, Costa Ricans have to pay a big cut on taxes, so much so that it limits their income and options considerably. The government suggests taxes every time they need more money, and still insist on keeping people in government positions sometimes earning more than the President of the United States. The Costa Rican government is a bureaucratic monster that is willing to eat his children and smile about it. The system was corrupt, impossible to overcome without illegality. I gave up on it years ago, for the sake of myself and maybe future generations. My brother thought the same way. Kevin agreed, but with a family to take care of and no legal way to access work in the U.S. it was impossible to take the leap. It didn't matter if he was a lawyer or a good, hard-working person. The inmigration system made it as possible to migrate to the U.S. as it was to win the lottery. In fact that was the name the U.S. embassy used to describe a contest for a visa in Costa Rica: the lottery, how fitting...

We stopped at the entrance of the cemetery. From the street, one could see miles of box-like tombs, all white. At the very middle there was a kiosk, a place to rest from the heat if one was assisting a funeral or visiting the dead. A small picket fence with well-kept bushes adorned the edge of the terracotta path across the cemetery. A small building at the entrance was the main operations center for the maintenance crew. There we asked about Alfredo's grave. The maintenance guy pointed at a modest but well-kept grave box, similar to the hundreds of other graves in the cemetery. There was nothing special about it, nothing that would tell the world he was a prince. It was a regular site with only one distinctive detail that made it different: the tombstone read "Alfredo de Prusia", no last name but the place where he was from.

"This is it?" said Kevin, sincere to the bone, as always.

"It appears to be," said Iris, trying to make sense of things. Something was off about the burial site. One would think that there would be a nicer, maybe marble, tomb at least. I remember visiting a cemetery by San José's Central Park, La Sabana, when I was younger. The tombs were extremely elaborate marble structures, some with statues worthy of royalty. Presidents and VIPs are buried there, and a walk in between Cementerio Obrero's isles is sure to put any ordinary cemetery to shame.

I bent down to pay respects to him. It was difficult to believe that the grave right in front of me was my father's. A stranger to me throughout my life, still it brought me sorrow to have a third parent under a pile of dirt. After some ten minutes I started to notice little things around the grave, like the flowers on the vase-like concrete ornament adjacent to the tumb.

"Sorry to bother you, man, but we haven't had breakfast," Kevin said after some time of reflection, not caring to interrupt what was a once in a lifetime moment for me. It was ok though, I was hungry too.

"Look, there's a small eatery right by the entrance," said Iris, as always already planning ahead.

"Good enough for me!" said Kevin as he walked towards the exit. Iris helped me get up and we followed his quick steps towards the *Soda*. As I was leaving his burial site I looked back and saw his grave further and further away, as if saying goodbye to the man I never met. A bittersweet goodbye, I would say, a combination of closure and an open chapter in my life that would never close.

We sat in the *Soda*, looking out at the memorial park, introspecting while looking at the white box-like burial sites. One after the other, the lines of unsuspected tombs were clearly different tones of white. Some were even almost gray from the lack of maintenance.

"Kevin, is there a specific reason why some graves are nicely painted and others are poorly maintained?" I asked as I tried to connect the dots together to form a clear picture of my long-lost relative.

"Yes, usually relatives and loved ones pay for the graves to be well-kept; the maintenance included by the cemetery doesn't include the grave itself, but the surroundings."

It made sense to me, after all, the same situation happens in the U.S, where the tombstones can be full of moss and mold, but have beautiful grounds around them. I looked at Alfredo's grave, and it was whiter than freshly fallen snow. Someone was taking care of his grave. It was good to know someone cared enough to remember him, even after death.

We were ready to ask for the check, when suddenly Iris pointed at the memorial park.

"Hey, guys, look!"

We saw what looked like a figure from far away, getting closer and closer to Alfredo's tomb. I instinctively got up and paid closed attention. As the figure got closer to the tomb, I got ready to run towards the cemetery, in hopes to catch at least a sight of who this person was and maybe find out why she still mourned my biological father.

I left the *Soda* as quick as I could, not minding the tab, and crossed the street as fast as I could. As I got closer, the figure turned into a female body, looking down on what was definitely Alfredo's grave. I went back into the graveyard and ran towards her. I slowed my pace as I got closer, since I didn't want to startle her. I was both excited and worried about how my conversation was going to go. It was definitely important to try to talk to her, but what if the information she gave me wasn't truthful, or worse, it was a truth that was too hard to bear?

"Buenas," I said to the lady, who was well into her senior years.

She looked at me, first as an imprudent, then perplexed.

"Alfredo's son!" She seemed to be very sure of who I was by just looking at me. I didn't know I was so similar-looking to my biological father. The resemblance had to be uncanny for a person to say it out loud to a complete stranger. She could be perceived as imagining things. But she was certain. So certain as to say it to my face.

"How do you know? Did you know Alfredo?"

She clearly noticed me confused, so she slowly got up. She cleaned the dust and dirt from her denim jeans, and said:

"It seems that this date is overdue. We have a lot to talk about."

She grabbed my arm, as confident of my good nature as a mother and her child, waiting for me to take her somewhere. I gently walked with her right back to the *Soda* table where Iris and Kevin were sitting. They were following me with their eyes as I approached the restaurant, until I arrived to take a seat with them. Kevin grabbed a chair from the vacant table on his right, and put it right next to the old lady for her to sit. Iris smiled at her and greeted her in Spanish.

"Hello, my name is Iris."

"Hi, Iris! I'm Isabel, a friend of Alfredo's, and now a friend of this handsome gentleman that brought me here." She looked at me and smiled.

"Oh, sorry! I'm Lucca, nice meeting you!" I grabbed

her with my left hand to help her sit, while extending my right hand to shake hands.

"Lucca! What a name! Very international!" She was surprised at my mom's selection. I didn't know her enough to understand if she liked it or not.

I introduced Kevin to her as my cousin from my mother's side. She was sweet and welcoming with every single word. She asked me about my mother; I regretfully gave her the news. She felt sad for my loss, but by her tone of voice I could tell she didn't know her very well. My suspicions were confirmed when she asked me about her life as if she were meeting a new person.

"Your dad..." she said, "was a very gentle human being."

We paid close attention as she told us the tale of Alfredo's father, Segismund of Prussia, and how he traveled to live first in Guatemala, where Alfredo was born, to finally settle in Costa Rica. She explained how Alfredo grew up in a country house that started as a modest home with some bee hives to produce enough honey to sell, until eventually Segismundo's farm achieved his dream of exporting honey to Europe. The sudden change in lifestyle was probably a harsh reality: the Prince and Princess of Prussia living in a small house with dirt floors and a wood stove. The business boomed, and so did the house Alfredo lived in, until it eventually had even its own library, with books from all over the world. Alfredo didn't seem to enjoy the luxuries; instead he would rather be outside, playing with the land that saw him grow. Eventually he was sent to study abroad with his sister Sofia. Segismund's only request was for Alfredo not to study in Germany, now under Nazi occupation, but instead to head to Switzerland. His sister Barbara, who had finished high school, decided to permanently move to Germany instead. Alfredo worked as any Costa Rican would have worked back in the day. He had several jobs, mainly organizing logistics, and one of those jobs was in Cachí, where he met my mother.

Isabel knew little of my mother; it was during a distant time where two soul mates collided in an inconvenient love affair.

"But, son, the most important thing for you to do right now is to call Jorge, his lawyer, because there are unresolved clauses in his testament that might be resolved with our chance encounter."

"What do you mean?" I asked her, concerned about the abrupt end of the story.

"I can't tell you because I don't know the details, but you should talk to Jorge," she explained while getting a piece of paper and a fountain pen from her purse. She wrote Jorge's contact info in what looked like old, cursive handwriting. She gave me the number and slowly left the table, crossing the street, back into the graveyard.

"Well, now you know who keeps the grave looking bright and white," said Iris as she broke the silence after Isabel's departure.

CHAPTER XIV

Just another day for you and me in paradise

We went on with our trip, heading now to the timeless Orosí Valley in Cartago. The day was still young, still promising each one of us what we were looking for. As we left the noise of the city into the mountains, the landscape changed into a combination of conifer trees and green pastures. The highway was in good condition for a Costa Rican street. Costa Rican streets are tedious; not only due to their unpredictable curves, but also because rainy season tends to be more like pouring season, washing away the street's asphalt layer. This phenomenom creates holes that become deeper with each passing storm, until eventually they become massive craters that take over the street. Highway "Florencio del Castillo" is made entirely of concrete, which helps to avoid the washing hazard of stormy weather. Concrete is expensive nevertheless, and paving every street with it becomes an impossible scenario when there are limited resources.

The radio went on as it usually is the case during a long trip, me as the driver, Iris as the co-pilot, and Kevin as the snoring friend in the backseat.

In Cartago, the oldest province of Costa Rica, the weather is a little cooler than the rest of the provinces. Cartago was the first capital city and the first settlement, therefore it has the most historic houses. Downtown Cartago has the ruins of an old church in the very middle. The church had slowly become a garden over the years, since it got destroyed by a powerful earthquake that also ruined most of the old city's structures. This trip however, was about Cachí, so I was told by Kevin to go through Paraiso, to make it a more scenic route.

Eventually we arrived at Paraiso. We stopped at the public lookout on our way to Cachí. The landscape was breathtaking; mountains as far as the eye could see, illuminated by sunbeams who casually chose to irradiate their light on specific points. It was the most accurate representation of God, the very definition of greatness and paradise. No wonder it was called Paraiso. The white farm-like fence was the only thing that kept us from flying into the sky. At least it felt that way. We spent a while admiring the awe of nature calling to us. It was primal, yet sublime. At the bottom of the landscape, one could see the Valley of Ujarrás. A small town filled with farmland that is legendary for its church ruins right in the middle of the valley. The ruins are like a mysterious muse, calling from every possible viewpoint in the trip. The green mountains and blue skies composed the most color-striking landscape. Once in a while, one could see small spots of red, almost like spilled paint on an immaculate canvas landscape. They were red torch gingers scattered around the fields and planted randomly in farm edges.

"This is outrageous," said Iris about the natural features of the place.

"It's so beautiful it's ridiculous, like an exaggeration that could never be true," she continued.

She had a point. It was scandalous, extravagant; like an overstatement or an unlikely hyperbole. Nothing one could describe in a conversation. Nothing a picture could capture, even if it was the most advanced camera. I hugged Iris, as part of the inspiration that wanted to take over my soul. Kevin was quiet, looking at everything. He looked at us and smiled.

"Let's go, people, so we can have time to go eat."

"We're we eating now?" I asked Kevin, since he

looked like he had a plan.

"You'll see," he said with a smirk.

We headed out and straight to Kevin's secret eating plan. We arrived at an unpretentious gravel main entrance that offered parking and access to an old brick house. Once seated, you could see the merit of the place. A house in front of a lake that had a terrace for outdoor dining. The flowers and vines surrounded the area, creating arches of blooms that framed the water view. On one side of the house there was a coffee plantation, with rows of coffee plants as far as the eye could see, sharing their space with mature trees that might be the saving miracle of a shade to a coffee plantation worker.

"If any of you drink coffee, this is the place to order it," said Kevin, who was having a blast every time us tourists wondered at something.

"I'll order a coffee then," said Iris to the waiter, who was already waiting for our order by the table.

"What natural juices do you have?" I asked the waiter. My mother taught me to ask this question all my life. She hated the artificial sugar in sodas, and thought that there was nothing better than to drink natural juices at least three times a day.

"Cas, limonada, mango, piña, guanabana en

agua,.." The list went on and on, which is usually the case. Restaurants in Costa Rica have a thousand natural drink options for a fraction of the price, compared to a natural juice stand in New York, which is both expensive and uncommon.

"Cas, please." Cas is a tart, round fruit from the guava family. It's addictively refreshing, although sometimes I wasn't too fond of the protein it might carry–A.K.A worms. Never mind that, I was too thirsty and already had it in my mind.

After a while she came with two empty jars and my cas juice. I knew what was about to happen.

"How strong do you like your coffee?" asked the waiter, to make sure he was placing the right amount of coffee inside the sock.

Kevin looked at Iris as to please her in the decision.

"Oh, I like it as strong as you can possibly do it," she instructed the waiter, maybe already numbed by the coffee she took during those long nights at the hospital.

Kevin was perplexed and uncomfortable about Iris's decision. He was sharing the coffee with her, and his stomach might not agree with what his pride was instructing him to do.

"Well then, let's add another spoonful," the waiter

continued.

The food was as great as the coffee, very fancy looking for such a country inspired establishment. Full stomach after feasting, we headed to the hydroelectric plant for the sake of my personal story. We were all full beyond measure of the visual grandeur of the Orosi Valley. Nevertheless we had a purpose on this trip, and Cachí's power plant was our destination.

We headed to Cachí's Power Plant. It is around 80 meters tall, but it's one of the narrowest hydroelectric plants in the country. Its blue gates command the landscape, and the massive concrete wall has no place to hide. The bridge that connects the power plant to the road vibrates with the passing cars. This movement, combined with the height of the bridge, tells me this is no place for acrophobia. The vegetation down below is still trying to climb up the walls of the plant, as if the very trees were afraid of Reventazon River's fury. Reventazon is the river that feeds the hydroelectric plant, but it is also well known amongst the people for its torrential currents.

Kevin mistakenly sensed a romantic moment and went a bit further away to avoid becoming an annoying third wheel. I heard his phone ring and saw his figure, now a bit smaller and monochromatic from the distance, answer his call. He moved his arms with aggressiveness, and

I could hear his upset tone, even though the noise of the dam was in full force. He looked down and touched his hair, resting his hand on his forehead. He ended the call and immediately changed his posture. Kevin crouched as if hiding his face in between his shoulders. He was looking down. Every single body gesture told me he just got bad news. I looked at Iris, and she was as concerned as I was about what we witnessed. I immediately ran to Kevin, yelling his name as if his soul was falling down an abyss and I wanted to call it out before it was too late.

"Kevin! Kevin! Are you ok? Do you need help with anything?"

I could now see his face; the curled brows, the tears in the eyes. He looked concerned. I felt unable to help him.

"Kevin, what's wrong?"

"It's Vera, she doesn't want me to go back home; she told me we're through."

Vera, Kevin's wife, was always a little feisty. I did understand why they fell in love though; she was the force and he was the peace. I thought they complemented each other very well. Lately, they argued often. He thought she needed space, but she kept pushing him further and further away. The relationship was complicated, not to mention his two small children. Vera was always a problem solver; her confrontational nature didn't allow for anything else. Kevin, on the other hand, was a procrastinator, especially when it came to feelings. He was there to help others, as I could easily attest, but when it came to his own mind, he just let everything pile up to the point of unsteadiness, even to the most patient partner.

"I'm so sorry, Kevin. Maybe she's temporarily mad, and she expressed it determinedly." I was trying to settle him down. Anyone could tell he still had strong feelings for her. He just didn't know how to fix this broken mess.

"I don't think so. She would get mad, but this is the first time she told me to leave."

"Have you talked to her to see what she wants?" said Iris from behind.

"What do you mean?" said Kevin, as if she was just not all there.

"My mom and my dad went through a rough time when I was a teenager. They almost got divorced. I remember my mom starting arguments for situations that wouldn't have bothered her before. My dad would just stay away from her to avoid confrontation, but it made her mad. When I talked to Mom, she used to cry. She would tell me my dad didn't love her anymore. He didn't make time to smile with her and do activities together that they both liked. She was mad because he wasn't there, not because of something he did."

Kevin touched his face as if he was kneading dough. He could be a reliable and agreeable person, but Vera could destroy his world with a simple comment. Especially if it involved the kids.

My phone was next in disturbing our situation. I wasn't going to answer, but because of the many calls avoided before, I felt a duty to answer the phone. I signaled Kevin to wait for me for a minute with my index finger, while Iris took my place in comforting his broken heart.

"Hello?"

"Hello, is this Lucca? This is Maxine, your late mother's lawyer."

Max finally made her debut in my story. She had been trying to contact me since Mom's passing.

"Max! I'm sorry I couldn't take your calls..." I wasn't done with my apology when she interrupted me.

"It's ok, Lucca, we all understand the reason behind your depression. I was sad myself, your mom was a good friend of mine and my dad's," said Max, telling me my apologies were unnecessary.

She continued with her information.

"As you know, your mom left all her legal instructions with our firm, and I wanted to show you what she left behind for your brother and you. Do you have the office number, so you can make an appointment?"

"I think so, are you in Quepos?"

"No, we work at the Escazú location during the week, and we head Thursday to Quepos to sign documentation and supervise the week's work."

"Oh, well. I'm at Escazú right now, all the way until Monday evening, when we head back to Quepos."

Max was open on Monday, thankfully, so we agreed to see each other Monday morning. My heart pounded by just hearing back on the subject of my mom's death. I guess I still had it fresh in my mind. I can still unconsciously bring back feelings about that day. I thanked Max for the after hours call and wished her farewell.

By then, Kevin gained a bit more composure and was back to at least his previous body posture. We decided to head back to Tita's house, after a long day of intense feelings and new experiences.

CHAPTER XV

Don't stop believin'

Monday morning was hasty, to say the least. I was still thinking about my mother and her untold past. I was still wondering about my biological father; what his tone of voice was, how he walked, things that couldn't be appreciated unless one personally knew an individual. The only thing left to do was to remember those who we knew instead of wishing to know the strangers in our lives.

I headed to Max's office. The way was quiet, since both Kevin and Iris stayed behind. My thoughts overwhelmed my head, thinking about the information Max was going to share with me. Mom did have her little piece of land, but the most disturbing thought of all was to think that she might uncover information about me and my past that I didn't know about.

I arrived at the office complex building

at 8 o'clock sharp. The building, a terracotta architecturally-rich structure, was as mystic as the information I was about to hear. The different water features helped the many conflicted guests go about their respective affairs. The openness of the lobby created a daunting echo, not very welcoming, but eerie enough to evoke a sense of formality within the visitors. The steps resounded heavily, one after the other, as anyone approached the front desk. I sat on the very modern furniture of the waiting area, which seemed to go in accord with the contemporary and pre-Colombian styles fused together in the building. Minutes later I was called to Max's office, up the second floor to the right.

Max was waiting for me with her very relaxed formality, hidden beneath her gray office outfit. Next to her was a senior gentleman, as ancient as Costa Rica itself, standing right next to Max with a cane.

"Hello, Lucca! I'm glad we were able to meet today." Max, an easygoing woman in her 40s, was one of my mother's closest friends. I didn't remember how they met, all I knew was that she was always there when Mom needed help. If it wasn't for her, I probably couldn't have beared living away from her for so long.

"Max, I never knew you were this high-caliber lawyer here in San José," I told her, perplexed at her surroundings. After all, back in Quepos she had a tiny office and wore loose dresses with flip-flops.

"Quepos is where I help, where my community is," she said.

"San José, on the other hand, is where I make the money to afford being a part of the community in Quepos," she continued. Apparently we were all migrants in one way or another. We all had our happy place. Some could afford the luxury of living were we wanted, at least part-time, like in Max's case.

"Fair enough."

She introduced the senior man as her father, who quietly greeted me so as to not disturb the course of the meeting. Max sat while fixing her blazer, and proceeded to explain my mother's wishes before reading the will.

"Before anything else, your mother also wanted your brother to be present. When he left for New York, she knew that wouldn't be possible, so she settled for a phone call if you agreed to the terms."

"Of course, for obvious reasons."

"Very well, let's call your brother. I took the liberty of setting an appointment with him yesterday after our phone call, so he's expecting us."

She grabbed the phone and dialed my brother's number through her land line. The phone rang three times before Renzo picked up.

"Hello?"

"Hello, Renzo, it's Max, I'm calling you to proceed with the reading of the will."

"Yes, proceed."

Max read the legal conditions of the will, followed by my mother's specific wishes. She reviewed her assets: her land, her car, her belongings. Renzo and I stayed quiet, attentive and serious, waiting for her to give us the information. My seat was comfortable, my legs crossed, my foot tapping quickly on top of my knee. My left hand touching my lips out of stress.

"Finally, all my assets, including my land and my car, will be given to Lorenzo Coto."

"Wait, what?" said Renzo over the phone, thinking that it might be a mistake to inherit the family house, even though he was the youngest brother.

I didn't know how to react. My mother gave everything to my brother. I felt anger out of her mistrust. I felt deceived one more time, as if there must be a very good reason to come to the conclusion that Renzo was better deserving of her possessions than me. Was it maybe because she felt I was irresponsible? Wasn't I enough to inherit at least part of the land? I honestly felt attached to Quepos, the land, its people. Maybe not enough to live there now, but maybe one day. Maybe it was just me being selfish or immature.

"That is it, gentlemen. Renzo, I appreciate your time..."

Renzo asked questions about the legal aspects about his new land, and the challenges he faced for not being able to leave the U.S.

While Renzo and Max agreed with the logistics of the paperwork to close the asset transition, I decided to call Jorge, the other lawyer involved in my life, as to redirect the feeling of impotence and do something about the situation. The office was big enough to have several conversations at the same time without interrupting one another, and if I waited to make the call later, my memory might play a trick on me.

I dialed the number and waited for an answer. The first ring, the second ring. Suddenly there was a third phone call in Max's office, ringing several times. I tried to ignore it, since I was too busy complaining about the outcome of my mother's will in my mind.

I saw Max's father slowly reaching for

something in his pocket. He held the cane with his left hand, and took his phone out with his right hand. He saw the call, staring with a smile before answering. Then Max's father looked at me as if he knew something I didn't.

Meanwhile, my phone was still ringing, waiting for the lawyer to answer. In that moment, everyone in the room appeared to move in slow motion. Finally I heard a familiar voice on my phone call.

"Hello!" said the lawyer, who also happened to match the lips of Max's father as he spoke.

I looked at Max's father, smiling at me, and realized I was calling him all along.

"What the hell!" I said out loud, breaking the formal decorum of the office.

I walked towards Max's father, pale as a ghost, still trying to put the pieces together in my mind. I hung up the phone and stared at him, fixed on the idea that he had information I wasn't aware off.

Max abruptly stopped the conversation with my brother, just to look at the scene of a clueless prince and his mysterious outcome.

"Jorge?" I asked the old man, still in disbelief. He looked amused, and said to his daughter:

"Maxine, I'm going to need the office now," as he put the phone back in his pocket.

"There's a reason why your mother didn't leave her property to you, Lucca," said Jorge, now clearing his throat as to declare to the world an amazing discovery.

He opened the file cabinet right next to the desk and pulled out an old file. His movements lethargic, his hand trembling from age. Little by little his fingers danced in the mountain of paper and files. "Alfredo de Prusia" said one folder sleeve.

"Lucca, your father was indeed Alfredo de Prussia, prince of the region of Prussia," he confirmed as a way to start the conversation.

"Most of your family is still residing in Germany. You have an aunt, nieces, nephews, cousins, and a very famous great-great grandmother: Queen Victoria of England."

I was so confused. How in the world would I be of such descent? I was an unemployed New Yorker with dead parents, in the middle of Central America. How could I, a random guy from a random place, be family with royalty? I never thought of powerful individuals as better or more important than anyone else, but that thought becomes a little useless once someone tells you that you're a prince, a descendant of Queen Victoria herself.

I sat back down on the chair as if letting go, throwing myself on it. By then, I was already staring at the ceiling, hoping for it to transport me into a different dimension, one where everything was clear and there were no more secrets.

"May I proceed with the reading of your father's will?"

I looked at him in consternation. This journey of mine had not only brought pain, but also the discovery of life. I didn't know how to react, though. Was it wrong to be excited? Was I supposed to be sad about a total stranger's death? Was I meant to mourn him, even if I never met him? Out of all these questions, I was able to utter:

"Yes, go ahead."

He read the will just as Max did. Max took her phone and walked out of the office, winking at me as if I was about to watch a circus performance. He started by listing the assets and Alfredo's wishes to random strangers, as if I knew and should care about all of those people.

"Finally," he said, "I leave the rest of my assets to my son and only predecessor; Lucca of Prussia, Saxony and Altenburg."

"Wait, what?"

Half of the information was a blurred memory in my brain, which was probably not working already from the anxiety of it all.

He read the assets as a house in New York, another in Escazú, and one property in Spain. He told me about my aunt Barbara, and her heirs to the throne. He showed me pictures of Alfred, and his father Sigismund. The picture on file was an exact match to Segismund's original picture, which my mother kept inside the tin box.

"That picture, I have seen before," I told Jorge, while hardly looking in the back of my mind for some confirmation.

"Your mother wanted you to know that this is your grandfather," Jorge explained in his deep, gaspy voice.

As he explained everything, he waved his cane once in a while, particularly when he saw the need to exaggerate a distance or the magnitud of the conversation. Suddenly it hit me, my mother also had that same cane in her house. I remembered because Kevin and I were goofing around with it when we found the tin box.

"That cane..." I said out loud, with the hopes of linking two pieces of information together.

"Oh, yes, the cane. It was a gift from Alfredo, as a sign of trust. Maybe that's why your mom has it, he trusted her too, you know."

He continued to explain the amount of wealth and responsibility I had now. As he finished the lecture, he asked me if I had any questions.

"I don't even know what to ask," I confessed, my mind not willing to make amends with the reality around me.

I signed some documents and thanked both Max and Jorge for their enormous effort in keeping the assets safe and for sharing the information.

"Wait!" said Jorge while lifting his hand, arm stiff, as a warning. He quickly handed me a copy of the documentation in a folder.

I headed back to Escazú, hoping to wake up and laugh at a weird dream. I did understand it wasn't a nightmare anymore. I was probably not going to have to apply for a job anytime soon. I now had not one but three places to live. My mother, though, was still out of my reach, and would be until it was my time to finally join her.

CHAPTER XVI

The story of my life

As I drove back to Tita's house, it came to my attention that this time, I was the one bringing positivity to Kevin. He was there when I needed him. He went out of his way to organize everything when I was emotionally unavailable. He did it without judgement, without sowing guilt. Maybe even to the expense of bettering the relationship with his wife. Perhaps she was on the brink of letting go, and if he was there for her one more time it could have healed wounds a bit.

I arrived at Tita's, whistling, carrying the tune of a beneficial karma. I was ready to tell everyone about the incredible journey and how it all came to an unforgettable outcome. I opened the door, and Kevin pulled me to the side, lifting his hand to demand silence. He was giving me a heads up, and told me to listen with his other hand. I could barely hear Iris talking to someone over the phone. Her voice was cracking from anguish, there was a detrimental event going on in her life. I could hear her repeat the word "daddy" and "dad" very often. She was interrupting whoever was on the other side of the line, and her voice was louder with every passing second, until she was almost screaming. She said a couple of sentences in anger, then she finished up the call with the typical "fine".

She hung up, and there was silence for a couple of seconds. Kevin and I looked at each other confused, awaiting another sign of emotional distress. We finally heard a sigh, and then sobbing. I got up and headed to where she was, in Kevin's old room. Her face was red, and her cheeks wet from the tears in her eyes. Her back was slouched, and she was still holding her phone with one hand. She was sitting on the bed, her eyes looking deep into the floor.

"Iris?" I asked, since I didn't know if she wanted me to know her problem.

Iris looked at me, cleaning her tears with the inside of her shirt. I happened to know that Kevin always kept tissues in a box on his desk, so I immediately grabbed one and gave it to her.

"Thanks, Lucca," she said while blowing her nose with it.

"Do you want to talk about it?"

I felt intense about what happened. For some reason I was enraged at whoever made her feel this way. I wanted to make the world a better place, to fix it for her to be smiling at me again.

"Well, that was my dad. He said the trip is over and I have to go back home."

"But aren't you supposed to stay for the summer?"

I couldn't understand why he felt she had to go back. Was it me? Maybe she told him about me and he became overly protective.

"May I ask why?" I didn't want to intrude with my question, but I couldn't fix the world if I didn't know what to fix.

She sighed again.

"My dad was laid off. He's afraid we aren't going to make ends meet, he's pulling the plug on anything that isn't necessary or generating income."

Iris was devastated. The love of her life was her career. She was a nurse first and foremost. Her patients were the most relevant thought in her mind. She thought of them morning, afternoon, and evening. She even went so far as to choose nursing over medicine because, as she said, "doctors don't have as much contact with the patient as nurses do".

"I understand. Is there anything I can help you with?" I asked Iris. After all, my mom always told me there was nothing worse than to be misunderstood. Sometimes people share their troubles not to find a solution, but to hear themselves out. The more they say it out loud, the better they can process the problem and find a solution to it.

"I guess we have to go back, so I can pack and change my flight. I honestly don't know how to deliver this information to my volunteering coordinator. I'm concerned he's going to complain to the program about it."

"If there's something I learned these past days, Iris, is to take troubles one step at a time."

"I guess so," replied Iris politely, with a soft voice as if she ran out of words.

"Is everyone ok?" asked Tita with a concerned and sweet voice. She was entering the room with the same face a deer might show right before a car crash.

I explained to her the situation, by which she furrowed her brows and gaped in disbelief. Her hands, both together as if grabbing our troubles to take them away. She called Kevin and told him out loud, Costa Rican style, right in front of Iris.

Suddenly we were all involved in Iris's struggle. The tiny room became a discussion arena where we all thronged, mumbling with determination to find the best solution to the problem. Everyone was debating whether or not to do something about it.

Iris looked at us all like if we belonged to a circus, and then diplomatically thanked everyone for caring. I guess we were about to see if Iris really was into Costa Rican culture.

We headed to Quepos immediately, Kevin still with us like a vagabond without a home. We were officially a gang. Temporarily, of course, but very aware of each other's strengths and weaknesses. I held Iris's hand the whole trip to Quepos. It was a goodbye that could end up as an average summer fling, or it could settle and become an eternal hello. I didn't know the future of this relationship, all I knew was that I didn't want to say goodbye. I was at a crossroads, but I had to find my way back home. By home I meant her; she was home. She was my ground, the reason I kept it real. My mind was working towards a plan, an idea on how to stay together.

"Iris, I might have an idea," I dared to tell her my plan, fearing for her to feel too vulnerable.

"Really? What is it?"

"Hear me out. What if we open a Go Fund Me page for you to finish your volunteering without your dad having to pay for it?" I was anonymously planning to donate myself, now that I was a secret millionaire.

"I don't know, Lucca. I don't feel like I should be a charity case."

She was right about one thing: seeing the level of poverty in some areas in Costa Rica, one couldn't easily find the perspective to say such things. After all, just by living in the United States alone she was probably considered to be in the upper class, compared to the rest of the world.

"I get it." I did, of course, but my plan was to help her myself, and her level of reality didn't help the case.

"How about you ditch your dad and find a job?" said Kevin without remorse. He truly wasn't concerned with how people might take his suppositions. I got where he was coming from, though. In Costa Rica there are several universities that are free for all. In fact, the best universities in the country are free. They are hard to get in nevertheless, and only people with high IQs might end up studying in such places. Forget about an essay convincing a panel of life experiences worthy of a spot in the school; in Costa Rica they base university admissions solely on test scores and an average grade of your last five years of high school –yes, high school is five years in Costa Rica, and there is no middle school. If you don't make the cut you're probably doomed to work and study at the same time, unless your parents save you from such stress by paying for college.

"Kevin!" I replied scandalized.

"It's ok, Lucca, he's just trying to help. But to answer your question, I can't really be in nursing school and work, let alone volunteer," explained Iris, with the patience of a ninety-year-old woman crossing the street.

"I'm not trying to be mean, Lucca. I'm just thinking out loud to see if an idea of substance comes to life." At least he understood he was just blabbing. We got along pretty well, considering the stressful circumstances we went through together.

"How about you, Kevin?" said Iris, turning the focus of the conversation towards his own mess.

"Honestly, I don't know what to do. I'm missing my kids already, and I bet they are asking for me."

He explained how he used to play "squishing machine" with his kids every night. He used to pretend he was some sort of heavy machinery and would roll around the carpet after a workday. The kids would jump on him to avoid being squished. They were young enough to find the jump challenging, so much so that they would scream out of excitement. Some days he was too tired and fell asleep on the floor as the kids lost interest and went away. Diego, his youngest, was the spitting image of him, not only physically, but emotionally. His temper, his sense of humor, it was almost surreal how a kid as young as four could be so similar to a parent.

"Vera still won't talk to me," said Kevin, looking out of the window but inside his soul at the same time.

The rest of the ride was mostly silent, each on his own set of difficulties. Kevin was working remotely whenever he found a good enough internet signal to connect. Iris was busy texting her friends about her issues. I was determined to find a way to help her stay. No one had asked about how my appointment with the lawyer went. I didn't want anyone to bring that up just yet, at least not until I could figure out a way to help Iris financially.

CHAPTER XVII

*Do you feel my heart
beating? Do you
understand?*

When we arrived at "El Retono", now Renzo's land, we waited for Ed to open the gate. He seemed happy in an intriguing kind of way. His eyes tattle-told a hidden story, and the rogue look of his facial expressions made me suspicious of his intentions.

"Pura vida, Ed. What's going on?" I asked him, my finger hard pressed on the window button. My shoulders went up, and I leaned towards the car door, as if my body would help open the window a little faster. He wasn't hiding his plot very well, either because he was a terrible actor, or because I was about to find out what he had in mind.

"Oh, nothing really, just doing my job!" he claimed, still not acting his part well. He walked towards the house with his hands in his pocket, silently laughing.

I looked at Iris to see if she noticed something was off. She looked back at me and shrugged, showing how clueless she also was. I closed the window and accelerated a bit to get into the house. Kevin was already wary on the secrecy in my life and randomly asked out loud:

"What's wrong with that dude?"

"I have no idea, but I'm too tired to figure it out, so let's just go inside," I suggested.

Iris decided to stay at home for a bit, since the internet access was better at the house than at her temporary apartment. She was dreading the video call she had to make to try to convince her dad to give her a week before returning. Iris wanted to look him in the eyes before he rejected her stay. She didn't want to lie to him, and still she was so tempted to tell him that the next available flight was a week from now. She understood her dad's anguish, of course, and obviously that kept her from selfishly deciding how to spend his money on herself. Iris headed straight to the terrace for a little more privacy. Nobody would hear her there; the house was set in the middle of a property that was never going to be developed, according to my mom.

I got out of the car, while Kevin unpacked

his belongings. I headed to the door, and as I got in I was able to see the tin box again on the table. I looked at it with nostalgia, thinking that not long ago it was a puzzle I desperately needed to solve. Funny how life was bringing closure to my dilemma. An unexpected type of resolution for sure, but the dramatic ending didn't take credit away from the journey and what I learned from it. I sat on the sofa to appreciate the items one last time before putting them away. The livery collar, the key, the admissions card; all puzzle pieces that already found a fit in the bigger picture. But there were still items that were a mystery to me. There was the letter, too faded to be readable.

"Lucca, get your stuff out!" said Kevin, already organizing himself to go to sleep. Kevin was not a heavy sleeper; he preferred to go to bed with everyone else to avoid waking from the noise.

I went to the car to get my bags and the paperwork that Jorge and Max gave me. I never checked what was inside that folder, maybe it was time to do that as well.

I left everything on the floor, still worried about Iris's conversation with her father. I wanted to be there when she came inside, regardless of the outcome. Suddenly, I heard the sliding doors that face the yard open and close again. I got up, hands in my pocket, waiting for her to discuss her father's wishes.

"He said a week, but no more than that." Her facial expressions were lifeless, no doubt she was still concerned about the time given. After all, she was supposed to stay for four months.

"Well, maybe we should consider other ways to pay for your volunteering expenses," I suggested, already planning on telling her my whole story.

"What do you mean?" she asked.

Out of nowhere I heard a bouncing, repeated sound in the distance. Then it was two sounds... and later a flow of sounds all together as water falling from a mountain into a deep lake. As I got closer to the front door I understood that there were guitars playing a melody outside. I looked at Iris as if maybe she wanted to surprise me, but she was as clueless as myself. So we both got out, thinking that maybe it was a mistaken address, but then again, why were they allowed in?

Outside, there was a trio, a set of three guitarists playing an old romantic song about a clock's unforgiving marking of time, and how soon a person would leave. Next to the trio was Vera, Kevin's wife, singing her heart out to the front door. Vera always had a great voice, this time it was no exception. I remember from my previous visits, when we used to go karaokeing. In front of Vera were Kevin's kids, all with toy guitars and warbling the song as they tried to follow along. Vera was dressed in a beige, long dress and flip-flops, her brown, wavy hair loose. As she saw me, she winked and kept vocalizing the romantic song. Iris hugged me and whispered in my ear she was heading inside to get the phone to record the unforgettable moment.

Out came Kevin, his hair sculpted with anti-gravitational force, probably from being in bed. He used a lot of gel, so any posture that smashed his hair for half a second made him look like he just came out of a war zone. Iris came right after, her video feature on her mobile phone already on, capturing the moment for posterity. Vera came closer to clueless Kevin, who not even a day ago could have sworn he was getting a divorce letter at any given time. Vera got even closer, as if she was going to trance Kevin into a deep romantic spell. Her eyes were closed for seconds and then back open when she reached a lower sound. She grabbed his hand and kissed his middle finger's knuckle, as she kept singing until the song finally came to an end. Kevin's eyes were red and watery, something his glasses couldn't hide. He touched the corner of his eye and cleaned the tears before making the crying official, and then took his glasses off and cleaned the lenses to avoid the mountain of feelings he was sensing.

"Come here you fool! Why did you leave?" said

Vera, embracing his emotions and his body at the same time. Kevin's two kids ran to hug their parents as well, almost climbing on top of them as the best exercise to perform at the moment. The trio guys, all smiles and positivity, changed the tune and the lead singer, so Vera could keep hugging the devil out of Kevin.

"But you said to not come back again!" Kevin was in disbelief to see all the public affection his wife just showed him.

"I said not to come unless you're ready to be open with me! And you just left!"

Iris and I were eavesdropping the whole conversation. It was like watching a romantic comedy's finale. Kevin's kids were already restless, so Iris looked at me and asked the kids if they wanted something to drink, just to take them inside and give the two lovebirds some space. Off they went, pretending to be airplanes, inside the house, still with their guitars strapped to their tiny bodies.

"But you were really mad!" said Kevin, still confused about what Vera was thinking.

"Imagine how I was when I found out you came to Quepos because 'I kicked you out' by my mother-in-law!" said Vera, still a bit mad but caressing his hair as to let him know everything was ok.

"I was just doing what you told me," said a repentant Kevin, looking down the floor, soaking in shame from his drastic measure.

"You're so sentimental, my love," said Vera, scolding him with a kiss.

"I'm sorry, I'll try to communicate a bit better next time."

After that I turned around and walked towards Iris and the kids, who were already playing with the tin box items.

I ran to safely store the objects, when Mercedes, the oldest of Kevin's children, grabbed the unreadable letter. She looked at me as if toying with my reaction, and slowly ripped the paper in two. Iris looked at me, gaping as if the paper was the source of her oxygen.

"Mercedes, why did you do that!" said Vera in a very different tone than the one she used to sing to Kevin. She ran to Mercedes from the entrance and grabbed her by one arm, pushing her towards a corner of the living room, where she scolded her for what she did. Mercedes got her arsenal of loudness out and cried with a high-pitched shriek, one could deduct where she got her voice from.

"I'm sorry, man," added Kevin, who was embarrassed already from the previous display of affection.

"What did she do?" he asked, not understanding it was a piece of the antiquities.

"It was the letter, remember, the unreadable writing?" I was already touching my head from frustration. Not that the kid understood what she did, but still, it was one of those priceless possessions of mine.

"Oh, man, I'm sorry, I know how irreplaceable it is."

Iris went to look for some tape to put the letter back together. As illegible as it was, I wanted to keep it available. If there's one thing I learned over the past days, it was not to take any piece of information for granted.

It was late at night, so Vera and the kids stayed with us at the house. The kids slept on the sofas, and I dropped Iris off before going to bed. I was planning on telling her about my good fortune tomorrow, so I asked her to come home so we could finish planning for her to stay the whole term of her volunteerism without becoming an economic burden on her dad. Hopefully she would accept my investment. I was going to be able to manage and stay longer in Costa Rica, so best-case scenario we could share some more weeks together.

CHAPTER XVIII

And we can build this thing together

Early morning I was awake, too excited, or perhaps worried about the information I was going to share with everyone. Maybe it was Mercedes, running around the hall, trying to get away from Vera's and Kevin's arms. Perhaps it was little Kevin, crying to get away from a diaper change or knocking at doors to make sure everyone "joins the party", as Kevin maliciously suggested his son do. It didn't really matter; I was just deep into the reality of a new day's challenge. I didn't want to go out the door, for I knew I had to stop a toddler from breaking something or find a kid who conveniently disappeared when called.

Kevin was cooking, as always. Vera was yelling, as always. It was the same dynamic as if they didn't fight and almost divorced (at least according to Kevin). On the other hand, Vera would tell a completely different story, on how her dramatic husband decided to take her over-emphasized grudge literally and resolved to leave her. They would probably laugh about the whole melodrama in 10 years and eventually tell it to their grandkids as a funny anecdote. Looking at them made me realize that life's imperfections usually are the reason for happiness; if life was always a certainty, how would a person ever get an adrenaline kick out of a thrill? How would one know what happiness is, if you have never experienced sorrow? The reason there are ups is because there is a mountain to climb in the first place.

With my shoes on and my hat on my head, I rushed out to pick Iris up. Unfortunately, I was caught up on a mountain of bouncing cheeks and baby saliva. As with every activity with children, first it feels like a hassle, and then it absorbs you until you become a kid yourself. I passed the fun and headed to the car, in a desperate attempt to be on time.

Iris was ready and waiting for some time, something she immediately forgot after I told her that her competition was a four-year-old little girl with brown, curly hair, and green eyes. She grabbed my arm, as if she was proud of my delay.

"I'm intrigued on how your story ends, Lucca," Iris stated as a conversation starter.

"My lips are sealed until everyone is at home."

"I'm not spoiling it, not even for you."

I turned the ignition on, and then I heard my phone ring, interrupting my trip.

"Hey, Lucca, it's Kevin, I was wondering if you could meet us at the marina instead. The kids are restless; that way we can pay more attention to what you were going to tell us." Kevin was right; before leaving, the kids were already hyper.

"Sure, let's meet there. I'm on my way; it'll be around ten minutes."

As we arrived close enough to the marina to look for parking, it took us a while to find a spot. I couldn't understand why, though, the marina wasn't this filled up during this time of the day.

We finally parket and walked to the Marina Pez Vela. The white, newer construction is a testament to what stereotypes can do to a place. Initially created for tourists, the marina's architecture screams high-standards, which made the locals skeptic about finding reasonable pricing in any of its establishments. This became a problem, so much so that the marina had to create an advertising campaign specifically targeting locals, announcing its good prices, in order to avoid the restaurants and shops from falling into bankruptcy. Eventually locals gave the marina a chance, and now they still lure customers with movie nights and other activities to keep the marina in good grace with the locals.

White buildings, together with native trees and decorative lightbulbs surround a green area where there was a conglomeration of people talking to each other as if the city's mayor was about to give a speech. There was Max, smiling at me from a distance, and Ed, who was supposed to be at the house guarding the gate. Kevin was gesturing me to hurry up and approach the crowd, as if I knew why in the world the whole of Quepos was gossiping and looking at us.

"There she comes!" Vera screamed at the top of her lungs. I was completely clueless at what was going on, but Iris kept looking at me as if I had anything to do with it.

"What's going on?" she asked as soon as she reached the crowd. Even the giant jellyfish ornaments hanging from the light green rooftops seemed to be complicit in this orchestrated plan. Kevin took center stage, and everyone became silent as soon as we were close enough to hear what the town had to say.

"As everyone knows, Iris's trip was going to be cut short due to her financial arrangement with her father," Kevin said out loud, something that might be too personal to share, who knows, no one asked her.

"And since this town is not about to let such a splendid nurse go back to New York and miss the sunshine…" He kept narrating, something that appeared to be guiding me and Iris towards the center of his speech.

"We all agreed to help her stay, so that she doesn't have an excuse to go back!"

Everyone clapped, as if there was some sort of conspiracy towards helping Iris stay.

"So, here it is, Iris, come closer to me!" The crowd went wild. Iris looked at me as if she didn't understand the reason behind such fuss. Iris had a very altruistic nature, so she considered helping others her job and not some over-the-top deed.

Kevin handed Iris a piece of paper and a can full of cash, while everyone clapped and smiled at her. Iris already got a grip about what was happening, so she covered her mouth as if there was no way she was going to let her amazement get out of her body. Kevin gave her the can and explained:

"People in the community wanted to help you out, so you could properly finish your volunteering experience. We certainly can use another set of hands at the hospital."

Iris's eyes got a bit like crystals, shinning clear tears that were about to drop. Kevin then gave her a check.

"Some people in San José also wanted to help, so we set up a donation account where people could invest in Iris's stay."

Iris couldn't believe her ears. There she was, a college student almost at the end of her studies, receiving help from the people she thought needed help in the first place. Although many of the people that helped were of humble means, none of them were poor. They all had abundance of love and care, enough to share, even if that meant not getting that Sunday ice cream or restaurant meal. They were happy with the outcome, glad to help. They felt purpose and relevance. They felt needed and heroic. That's what abundance was about. It wasn't about material means or a competition to see who gets to have the best car or the biggest house; it was about giving when you could and receiving an act of kindness when in need. The best of humanity, exemplified by a simple humbling experience.

Iris cheeks were already wet with tears of joy, something many people haven't experienced in a lifetime. She grabbed the rusted can and the check and hugged everyone that got close to her.

Even Dr. Chang was there, Iris's boss, hugging her and crying like she was her own daughter receiving help.

I got close to Kevin, trying to figure out what just happened.

"It was Mom," Kevin whispered in my ear.

That slow moving grandma from Escazú decided to also be useful when someone else needed help, and called everyone during the four-hour trip we had to Quepos. She knew many people, and was able to organize an "Iris Stays" marathon. So many people helped in so little time, that it was almost as if the community was always on high alert, scanning the city to see who needed an act of kindness.

"Tita did this?" I asked Kevin, making sure I understood.

"Mom always gets what she wants, and what she wants right now is for you two to be together, because apparently she thinks you are a match made in heaven." Kevin laughed as he made fun of Tita's romantic.

The crowd spreaded towards the exit, some went on to the various shops and restaurants, others went down the steps to see the yachts.

I got closer to Iris and asked her how she felt:

"I'm in love with this place. I'm in love with its people, its land. All I have felt since I got here is love. I'm so grateful for this experience."

"Don't you consider it rude or intruding what Tita told others to create the fund?" I asked Iris, genuinely curious as to why she wasn't upset.

"Well, Lucca, I don't think it was ill-intentioned, and to not appreciate her gesture would be arrogant on my part."

It was funny how I was supposed to be the one saving her from the situation in my mind. I was the one who was going to figure out how. I was going to tell her I could give her the money, or let her borrow it, if she was stubborn enough. I wasn't counting on the ability she had to make people fall in love with her, and how much support she already had without me. I guess I really was there just to love her after all, the rest she obviously got.

CHAPTER XIX

*It's a new dawn,
it's a new day*

We arrived at the house after sunset. Kevin's kids were already sound asleep in the car, probably from the excitement of everything that happened at the marina. Iris was still smiling from her experience, looking out into the dark landscape as something to record in her mind. But it was my turn now. It was the moment of truth, when I was supposed to tell everyone my journey.

So, one by one, like a religious procession, each of us entered the house that once again became the epicenter, this time of excitement rather than grief. We all sat on the living room set, with the exception of Vera, who was putting the kids into one of the bedrooms. By then, it was apparent I had concealed information, and they couldn't wait any longer to figure it out. Kevin was staring at me as a kid when he knows someone is in trouble. Iris was just coming out of her magical experience into the land of "what's next". Vera was coming to the hall already, toes first, making sure no one was going to spoil her attention to what I was about to say.

I previously got the folder with the information on the inheritance out of the car, in case I forgot some detail on the subject. As they were all waiting in silence for me to make my first statement, Kevin decided to speak.

"For crying out loud! Get on with it already! We all want to know how it went!"

We all erupted in laughter, either because we didn't enjoy each other's company without the informality of a friendship, or because we were so filled up with happy chemicals from the previous experience that we didn't know what else to do.

I cleared my throat, placing my fist on my lips, to change back to a more serious tone. So I began to explain.

"Well, it happens that my mom decided to leave this house and the rest of her assets to my brother." I smiled to make sure they understood I was ok with the decision.

Kevin frowned, feeling there was more information than what I stated.

"But…" I said, elevating my tone, as to rest the pause that caused commotion,

"I get my father's assets."

"You mean your dad had separate assets?" said Vera, completely clueless about the situation. After all, she wasn't communicating well with Kevin for a while.

"Vera, do we have a treat for you!" said Iris, while updating her with uncanny speed. Vera seemed to understand every single sentence that came out of Iris's mouth. I went to the kitchen to get something to drink and some cups. By the time I came back, Vera was up to speed and willing to give her opinion on the matter.

"As I was saying, I'm the sole heir of my father's assets, and he made sure there was a legal document that stated his last wishes."

"But, what are they, Lucca?" asked Kevin, impatient for such an answer since the very beginning.

"Well, first of all, officially my name is Lucca of Prussia, Saxony and Altenburg," I corrected Kevin. Iris, Vera, and Kevin reacted to my new name in three different ways, like monkeys giving a philosophical message through gestures. Kevin raised his brows, and his mannerisms explained how pompous I just sounded. Vera opened her eyes as wide as the sea we just came from visiting, grabbed her curly hair, and pulled it around her face like a psychiatric patient. Iris laughed while slapping her thigh, just by looking at everyone's reaction.

"Second, he left me three different properties. One in Escazú, another property in Spain, and a property in New York." I wasn't done bragging about my new status when Kevin reacted.

"Sounds fantastic, Lucca. Don't get this the wrong way, but that doesn't sound like the Kaiser of Germany to me. It sounds more like the assets of a distant cousin. I'm glad you have so much more now, but are you sure that's all he had?"

Kevin's statement got me thinking, first because he was right. The amount of wealth that the German aristocracy carried up to this point didn't match my newfound inheritance. Second, Kevin's statement made me realize there was some sort of dissonance between my title and the amount of assets. Maybe I had to know more about it to understand the situation.

"Kevin, let the guy enjoy his bounty! He's not even past the temporary joy of winning the lottery, and you're already making him unhappy about it!" said Vera, standing with her hands on her waist, scolding Kevin. Kevin apologized with a gesture, just by moving his mouth towards his ears, almost as a dog when it smiles. He also looked backwards trying to dodge his wife's disapproval.

"He's kind of right, though, did the lawyer give you any paperwork?" asked Iris intuitively, being the analytical type.

Iris reminded me of the folder Jorge gave me right before leaving his office. The folder was already in my hand, so I opened it and spread its contents on the coffee table, like it was a shareable appetizer anyone could try.

"Here, feel free to read," I offered everyone. In reality it was my way of asking for help.

We each grabbed a document from the pile. Everyone oblivious to a sealed letter that carried my name handwritten on the envelope. I guess it looked too personal to open, so I figured it was probably some sentimental wishes from Alfred, or maybe an explanation on why he was never around. I let the letter be, sensing its personal nature, and went ahead to analyze the rest of the documents that appeared to be of legal use.

Vera grabbed the document that was read by Jorge, only to figure out little Mercedes was calling for mama. She dropped the document and headed to the bedroom as automatic as a robot who received a new command. Iris grabbed it instead and read all the way in silence, pacing around the living room. Sometimes she stopped and thought on what she read for a few seconds, and then resumed her walk. Kevin grabbed another sheet of paper, one that I hadn't seen before, and sat on the couch like if no one else needed to rest comfortably on it. I read my mother's will again, just to make sure everything was correct. Almost by telepathy, Renzo called me to talk about it.

"Hello?"

"Hey, Renzo! Congratulations on your new property! I hope you don't mind me using it while in town?"

"No worries, go ahead! Anyway, where are you going to set your entrance to yours? I mean, my plan is to keep mine, so we're probably going to be neighbors." Renzo's chat was completely baffling me.

"What do you mean?" I asked, while checking Mom's will to see if there was some sort of misunderstanding on my behalf. Maybe she did leave me some land, but I was too anxious to even understand the information I received that day.

"Your property! The jungle surrounding Mom's house!"

"I don't have the slightest idea of what you're talking about. As far as I'm concerned, Mom left everything to you." I was still a little over emphatic about the statement, given the fact that my subconscious still remembered how I felt when I thought my mom forgot about me.

"I just rechecked Mom's inheritance, and it states that everything is yours."

"The land around Mom wasn't hers, Lucca. It was yours. It has always been yours."

I grabbed all the documentation and one by one checked to see if there was a legal document pertaining to the land around the house.

"How do you know?" I asked Renzo, since he seemed to be the one knowing about my life more than myself. I really thought I had it all figured out: the secrets, the clues, the relationships. It seemed to be a never-ending hole of conspiracy theories and information.

"After the reading of the will, I felt you were a little restless over the information, so I asked Max if she knew why Mom gave me the whole property to myself. She chuckled and said that the rest of the mountain was under your name since Alfred purchased the land for Mom, right before she got engaged to my dad."

Quepos made sense now. No wonder Mom let us get in and out of the mysterious neighboring property like if she knew no one would care. I felt like such a rebel when trespassing into the jungle with my friends. Now I realized my actions were inconsequential, just a naive teenager visiting his own land.

"Oh, now it makes sense," I replied to Renzo in a monotonous voice, almost as if it was expected for life to surprise me yet again. Not that I was complaining about it, but I felt a little embarrassed over my little tantrum at the lawyer's office. Now that I had all the information, my rush to leave Max's office felt unjustified.

Iris and Kevin were staring at me with their hands a bit in the air, asking what was going on with my life now. Vera arrived at the scene only to discover something new just happened and she missed it again.

"Now what happened?" she complained, slapping her thigh.

"Well, apparently there are now four properties under my name," I explained to them as if giving a Ted talk to an audience.

After hanging up and giving everyone the information, they were all amazed, understanding now why Mom never had an issue with her neighbors.

"I knew there was more!" shouted Kevin, making

sure nothing was amiss.

The rest of the evening we discussed hypothetical scenarios, and looked into a maps app to figure out where every single location was on the map. I still thought about what Kevin said, even when everyone was getting ready to sleep. I decided to get the tin box out and look at all the pieces of information Mom left to whoever was able to penetrate the wall. Each of the items was part of a road map to find something about my past and my future, all laid at just the right time, as if life was looking out for me in the long run.

CHAPTER XX

We didn't start the fire

It was early morning in Quepos. The morning dew was still resting on the flora outside the house. Far away, one could hear the customary rooster call from the country neighbor. The hummingbirds were feeding from an old feeder my mom placed by the balcony. It reminded me of her recent passing; the nectar was still sweet, still there, like her essence in this house. The weekend was back on my timeline. The sun was rising, and I was already making plans: I wanted to inspect my new acquisitions, one by one.

The successful fundraising event allowed Iris to stay in Costa Rica. The main reason she allowed herself to use the funds was her own charitable nature; she had been the helper herself many times and felt the pride of those who refused help often. Now ashamed to ask her to fly back home, her father realized his lack of funding was nothing compared to almost any of the anonymous donors at the fundraiser. He felt embarrassed that his daughter was in such distress and with such conviction that she received money from strangers, while he debated if he should sell his 2019 model car and exchange it for something more modest. She was staying for at least a solid month before heading back to Brooklyn. I promised her I wasn't going to peek at the properties without her; she was excited to see them with me, so we appointed this weekend as our first house visit.

The house was a mystery itself since the maps app didn't show a clear picture of it. One could only see vegetation and tile roofing from the main road, all covered with moss in between tiles. The vegetation was different from Quepos, like if it were the Orosí valley all over again. Kevin was meeting us at the disclosed address with Vera and the kids, now that they were back to being inseparable.

Iris arrived home mid-morning, ready for the four-hour trip to San José-west. She kissed me as if it was the most common gesture in the world, grabbing my wavy hair with her hands.

"I love your hair, the texture and the volume, very sexy," Iris said while winking at me.

"Are you harassing me?" I teased her since she knew that I was the one usually relentlessly following her.

"Only if you want me to."

Iris always had these clever comeback jokes, even from perspicacious Kevin, who almost read everyone's mind with his comments.

We went on with our trip, this time singing

together and holding hands. We were in a good mood, feeling a sense of achievement and grateful for life's outcome. We felt we could take over the world while sharing a strong bond with each other, formed over our respective misfortunes.

We finally arrived at Escazú, as slow as always, where Kevin was waiting for us at the old town's central plaza: a small, one-block green space filled with pavers and tall trees. Every Saturday, the park will become a spectacle of fruits and vegetables with its farmer's market. Farmers from all around Costa Rica would come to place a stand within the four blocks to sell their produce. The fruit was as fresh as it gets, and the variety included crops not seen in a usual American grocery store. Vendors would have a machete close by, and at the mere interest in a purchase, they would offer a piece of their product to the prospective buyer. One gets out of the market with a full stomach and tired of carrying the delicious purchases throughout the event. Since it was a Saturday, we decided to get the market experience before arriving at the property.

"Iris, come here!" I called Iris, who was already lost in a sea of colorful produce.

"Try this one, its called *Jocote*, one of my favorites growing up."

Jocotes are a small, round fruit, good with salt if it is still green. If the jocote is ripe, it is sweet and delicious, tight on the outside and full of yellow pulp on the inside. Either way, they are a delicacy and very traditional to Costa Rican culture.

"Careful, though, it has a big seed in the middle," said Kevin, probably thinking like a parent.

The tart flavor made Iris frown a bit. She was amazed at the loud sound that came out of her bitting, very characteristic of jocotes.

"This is so good! I love it!"

"I want some!" said little Mercedes, not understanding the danger behind the seed of a bite-size fruit.

"Not yet, honey, you might choke, and what would Daddy do without you?" said Kevin, showing his very paternal side. Iris looked at me as if Kevin were her pride and joy. Vera just laughed and said:

"That was cute, alright," sealing the compliment with a kiss on his cheek. Secretly she also grabbed his buttocks, but we didn't notice at the moment.

Little Kevin's stroller, a massive two-seat gray vehicle, was getting in everyone's way, so we quickly purchased some jocotes and continued our journey. Iris kept trying everything and buying whatever she could eat raw, amounting to a very tired Lucca. What can I say? I have strong arms, but the sun and the weight were a little too much for me.

"Are you tired?" said Kevin, winking at me, conveniently showing me how he used one of the stroller's seats and the storage area to fill up with kilos of fruit without exhaustion.

"This is so good!" interrupted Iris, showing her excess of dopamine from her tasteful adventure. That's how I spotted her every time she got lost in the sea of people walking up and down the street.

It seemed that the entire neighborhood attended the event, and Iris was oblivious to the struggle I had. It was an impossible task to follow her among the sea of customers with the produce weight on my arms.

Even though life at that moment seemed like a noisy mess, it was radiating joy to everyone experiencing it. We were all happy together, doing a fundamental act of everyday Costa Rican life, having a Pura Vida moment. It wasn't just us, though; everywhere you looked, there were smiles and laughter, producing a contagion of positive energy. All it took was the right attitude towards strangers, an understanding heart, a willingness to interact thinking the best in people.

"We should head to the house, guys," said Vera, already tired of pulling the stroller and asking for space to move on. So, we all nodded and walked out of the crowded street towards the cars.

The house was some ten minutes away towards the mountains, in San Antonio de Escazú, very close to Tita's house. As we approached the property, we realized there was a car parked on the side. The house was a historic property, so old that it was constructed entirely on *"bajareque"* or a combination of mud, clay, and straw. This traditional way of building houses dated from before concrete was ever introduced in the country. It provided fresh interiors during the day and warmer temperatures at night when the heat was released after the day's heat absorption. Bajareque houses were usually painted white, with a wide blue stripe around the bottom wall section of the property. This dark-colored paint served to avoid the mud from the rain to stain the white color of the house.

"I think there's someone there," whispered Iris, scandalized by what we considered an intrusion in private property.

"Whose house was this before it became yours, Lucca?" asked Kevin, who was walking with me towards the main door.

"My dad's, or so I thought,"

"Maybe we should call Max; she would be able to look at the registry," said Kevin.

"I'll call Max. You guys go ahead and knock at the door," proposed Iris while going back to the car.

"I'll text you the number," I replied.

Kevin and I looked at each other as if the weight of the world was on our shoulders. We walked slowly and stealthily, expecting the worst. Kevin could hear people laughing inside the house, and the window did show shadows moving behind the curtains.

Ding, dong.

The bell rang inside the house. Everyone in the house went quiet, and someone slowly approached the door. Kevin and I looked at each other as if we were about to burst from the mere thrill of waiting.

"Buenas noches, ¿en qué le puedo ayudar?" Out came a man in his mid-60s, full mustache and a slim body, very personable and educated, noticeable by the way he spoke. I learned how to notice how an educated person speaks in Costa

Rica. Every country has its own code regarding manners, particularly those that suggest you are a well-educated individual. There's a tone to the voice that changes, and the vocabulary used is also different.

I could almost hear Kevin's soul breathing out relief as if he felt he could discuss the current occupancy issues with him in a more civilized manner.

"My name is Lucca. I'm the new owner of the property. How are you?" I asked the very proper man as I extended my hand for a handshake.

The man's face changed after my greeting. He caressed his thick mustache with his left hand, a sign of a newfound worry. He then extended his hand as a courtesy in order to not leave mine waiting to be greeted.

"Good evening, Lucca. How are you doing?" He kept his cool and his better understanding of human interaction by inviting me in. I looked at Iris from afar. She was also making a worrisome face, maybe due to her phone conversation or how uncertain the current affair was.

Inside there was a big family meeting. Maybe they were celebrating an event; perhaps they all lived there. At that point, I didn't know. All I could tell by simple observation was that they were family, all right. The males were all a sort of variation from the tall, hairy man that opened the door.

"People, this is Lucca, the new owner of the property," he introduced us with a magnifying voice.

They all looked at Kevin and me as if we were aliens who just arrived from outer space. Like if we had visited the wrong house, but they were still going along with it.

"Hi!" said Kevin with a defeatist tone; no doubt he was a bit intimidated due to their numbers.

"But wasn't the house Ivo's?" said a woman who appeared to be the man's wife.

The man looked at her and secretly communicated mandatory silence, like he could take her voice and conveniently store it away while we discussed his living conditions.

"Who's Ivo?" asked Kevin, who wouldn't risk silence for the sake of comfort. He asked what we needed to know without regard to anyone's feelings or thoughts, for that matter.

There was an odd, quiet moment after the question, which served the purpose of me reading Iris' text message:

"Someone is using your biological dad's name as his to collect money from the house."

"Look, I don't mean to cause trouble, but I can tell you right now that whoever rented this house to you wasn't the rightful owner of the property, unless he had a legal document that said so," I replied to the man with an imperative tone, now suspecting a shady deal.

"What's your name again?" said Kevin, already noticing the lack of information.

"Martin, but people call me Ponti." I still don't understand why people will introduce themselves with their nickname as if such informality would be a good practice with the first conversation.

"Well, Martin, my girlfriend just called my lawyer to understand what's going on, and she tells me that someone is using my late father's name to collect rent without permission." Everyone's faces went from plain attention to scandalized. Martin's wife exclaimed a religious phrase, and the rest followed through with similar responses.

"We don't want any trouble. What do you suggest we do?" said Martin.

"Don't panic; I don't mean for you to feel unwelcome in your own home. I'll give you my number, so you can call me to set the payments to the right account. I'll deal with this Ivo character myself," I explained to Martin, making an effort to sound more as if giving instructions instead of suggestions.

"Ok, here's my contact information, Lucca; we appreciate your help. Just to make it crystal clear, can you send us a copy of your legal document that verifies your claim over the property?" That question made me realize they were afraid but willing to do the right thing. It made me realize it wasn't their fault.

We exchanged numbers and headed outside, and as I left, I looked at Martin in the eyes and placed my hand on his shoulder:

"Don't worry about us. We mean no harm. We'll figure it all out."

We left with that expression of good faith, heading into our cars as quickly as we could. Once inside the vehicle, Kevin called me from his phone to figure out the next step.

"Now what?"

"Now we talk to this Ivo guy."

"Maybe we should talk to Max first so we can understand the legal implications of everything before making a move?" Iris interrupted with her glorious piece of advice, as always.

"Let's visit her. Do you know where she is?" I asked.

"She said she was working until late today, so maybe her office?" said Iris, already grabbing my hand as brazing on something before a hard hit.

"Are you ok?" I asked her while kissing her hand.

"It's ok; I just don't like how this is going." For the first time, I wasn't the pessimist of the conversation, but Iris was. I intended to pay her patience for me with the same kindness I felt from her during my darkest moments.

"Everything will be ok. Worst-case scenario, I have to live out of two property incomes instead of three. It is still a pretty good bargain."

"I guess so," she said grabbing my arm and holding it with her body. She placed her head on my bicep and rested, just as I used to see my mom and dad do when we were traveling as kids. Maybe they also were trying to solve life's predicaments and gave comfort to each other that way. I thought as a kid it was only them loving each other, but there's more to it than just senseless affection. Love, after all, goes beyond physical gestures.

We went immediately to Max's office, which was relatively close by, even though it took us a long time to get there due to traffic. Max was expecting us already since we asked her for an emergency meeting regarding the subject. Kevin switched cars and rode with us since the kids needed a break from the long trip. Vera was also exhausted, and she wanted to head home with them. Kevin was full-blown hypotheticals in the vehicle.

"What if that Martin dude is actually a bad guy taking advantage about the fact that no one was asking for rent? What if there isn't an Ivo dude?"

"What if he's not, and he got played as badly as whoever was in charge of the property?" suggested Iris, aiming at relieving tensions between the parties.

"Let's not assume anything until we talk to Max," I suggested as a way to make peace between our anxiety and our future.

We arrived at Max's office at a hurried pace, me and Iris holding hands, secretly wishing we had the superpower of making things right if we held each other. Max was already cleaning up her desk to leave.

"Hi Max, I'm glad you haven't left. I need your help."

"Hello, Lucca, I'm glad you came."

We shook hands and sat wherever we found a place. Iris sat on the window sill, looking out. Kevin on one of the additional chairs placed against the wall. Max was already wearing her motorcycle outfit to leave the office, something many Costa Rican's learned how to do to avoid the terrible traffic jams. It isn't as safe as riding a car, but it does take you a lot less time to arrive home.

"So, what's the information you have so far about the situation with the house here in Escazú?" I asked.

"Basically, what my dad told me is quite an unfortunate story, to say the least."

In that moment, cold drops of sweat fell over my back, hiding behind my clothes, as a vivid reminder that the waves of angst can arrive at any given time and tumble you down from your comfort zone.

"There's a charlatan called Ivo Solano. He took over your dad's identity as asset manager months after his death. He waited for just the right moment: right after we checked on his assets to secure them. He then rented the property in Escazú. Gossip says he also tried to steal business from your land in Quepos, thinking it was under your dad's name. He desisted when he realized the owner was still alive," Max explained to us with a disapproving face while her hands were busy packing files inside her backpack.

"What can we do about it?" asked Iris.

"Well, you can sue him and press charges, but you have to be careful. Ivo is involved in some pretty dark ventures; some even say he has a hand in organized crime."

My jaw dropped to the floor. My dilemma wasn't an

innocent quest over my own life. It was about to get dangerous, and I didn't know if I was ready to face such extremes.

"Let me know what you decide to do. I can help you with any path you decide to take."

"Thanks, Max, I appreciate it. I'll let you know soon."

Deep down, I already knew what I was supposed to do. I needed time, not to figure out my next step, but to get my mind and feelings to agree with each other. Iris looked into my eyes and understood. Kevin was the only one with a bit of common sense and not emotionally involved to the point of desperation.

"So, hypothetically, if we set a legal route, what are the possibilities?" he asked, just to get a better understanding of what waiting could look like for me.

"It could take months for us to submit the issue to court. It extends if he doesn't want to let go of the assets with a warning, to the point where there could be a formal trial."

None of it sounded like immediate economic stability to me. The house income could take months to become legally mine. The land was just land, and land in Costa Rica could take years to sell.

"Do you know if the properties in New York or Spain are under the same duress?"

"I don't think so. He would risk being labeled as an international criminal, and that involves entities that would definitely expose him. Let me make some calls tomorrow, and I will let you know."

"All right, talk to you tomorrow, Max."

Kevin and Iris also said their goodbyes, and we headed out of the office. After that serious conversation, we were all quiet for a while, analyzing what could go wrong in our minds. The evening rain was pouring, making mirrors out of puddles. I could see myself inside the wet holes of the road: a reflection of a man whose crossroads once again had given him a choice to fight or to let life take its course. As I got deeper into my own thoughts, I heard a voice:

"Lucca, it's ok."

Iris, who was already seeing my signs of anxiety, had once again reminded me that we could go through it, no matter what happened. I let my jaw relax, since my teeth were already grinding. Iris noticed little by little what I tried so hard to hide: I get nervous, for the silliest things, sometimes without a cause. It started when my father died. He was my rock, my safety net. When I was in trouble, or when I didn't know what to do, a conversation with him would calm any doubts of a clear path to take in life. After he died, I felt an enormous responsibility and a sense of overwhelming stress. Little by little, as I saw my mom recover from his death, it became less frequent. But whenever life became complicated again, my anxiety spiked in seconds. It was almost as if my brain couldn't avoid heading towards a preordained path, one that was established during my father's death. Sometimes, when I had a busy day, such as today, my head would feel feverish, and my jaw would be in pain after grinding my teeth without knowing. So, now I was again, trying to decipher which decision was the best while at the same time trying to avoid the mentality behind a panic attack.

CHAPTER XXI

Is this love that I'm feeling?

On our four-hour trip back to Quepos, Iris asked me a very personal question: "Do you suffer from an anxiety disorder, Lucca?"

"To tell you the truth, I'm not sure," I replied, introspecting, trying to look inside myself for signs that might give me an answer.

The corner of my eyes braced as my mind put an effort to truthfully answer that age-old question. I tried to explain it to Iris, how my nerves would get a hold of me, body and mind, when I was under stress. Sometimes to the point where my decision-making process became paralyzed in fear. Iris was listening without judgment, without a self-righteous attitude that would make me feel rejected. Her attitude towards my weakness awoke in me deeper feelings towards her. This soul-searching exercise brought us closer. She made me feel loved and understood. It planted in me a seed of desire to become a better man. I needed that feeling to move forward in life; it inspired me to forge bravery within myself; enough of it to create a hero. In reality, she was my hero too, because she had the patience to articulate the right questions and follow-up answers. It was an almost sacred dynamic that made me feel we could conquer the world.

We arrived late as always to Quepos. It was only me and Iris. Kevin and Vera stayed behind with the kids. Iris fell asleep for the last portion of the trip, making it difficult for her to get off the car to her place.

"I'm so sleepy!" said Iris, once she heard the car's engine finally turn off. It got me thinking about the great opportunity of spending more time with her.

"You can always spend the night," I told her while casually kissing her forehead. I didn't want her to think I was planning a sexual encounter like a mysogynist man.

She thought about it for a few seconds, then, while asking for my hand to get her exhausted body up from the vehicle's seat, she agreed.

Iris walked a couple of steps like a destitute begging for water in the middle of the desert. Her legs seemed to carry a lifetime's load on them. I picked her up to deprive her of such martyrdom. I wasn't entirely selfless, though; I also wanted to be in bed since entering Parrita, more than an hour ago. I grabbed her from behind and lifted her without notice, which startled her so much that her eyes opened as wide as an owl at midnight.

"Sorry, I didn't intend for you to wake up."

She smiled and hugged me by the neck. Her hair,

now right within smelling distance, had a fruity scent.

I opened the door and went directly to the sofa. By then, Iris had become an over-weight to this pseudo-transport that were my arms. I unintentionally dropped her on the couch a little too rough because of it. Such wrongful way to lay her majesty to rest provoked a sarcastic laugh from Iris; this mere action was a derision to a perfect moment, a spark extinguished by the sudden outpour of rain.

"Wow, Lucca, how romantic," she sarcastically said while still laughing.

"I didn't know you wanted me romantic, Iris." I smirked, implying she was the one suggesting a different mood.

I got closer to her, and she did the same. Iris then held my hand and toyed with it while looking at me with her extravagant brown eyes.

"You know, Lucca, when you look at me with those thick brows and your blue eyes, it reminds me of why I love the ocean. It's almost as if you are a vivid reminder of this paradisiac place. Your brows are nearly the color of the sand; your eyes could be the perfect match to Manuel Antonio's ocean."

"Are you feeling inspired, Iris?"

"You inspire me, yes."

With that outrageous remark, Iris kissed me while my hands, restless from passion, went on looking for her waist. Her small shirt would move back and forth the movement of my hands holding her until I could eventually feel the goosebumps on her skin as my palms touched her back. My hands headed up her spine into her hair while she twisted her face to reveal her unforgettable neck. She smelled like coconut; this paradisiac place was already part of her. I kissed her again and again until my mere desire to do more made me lift her up back to the couch that she was on a few seconds ago. This time, though, I was on top of her body, covering her as a cave where she could take refuge. My hands, now misplaced after such mischief, went instantly to try to feel her again. She was very willing to follow through, an obvious deduction after feeling her own hands touch my back all the way to my buckle. I took that move as a sign for something more, so I lifted her shirt off. She helped me out with her body movement, a repetitive sway that could easily read as a future night of passion. Her neck and lips still hypnotized my mouth, but my hands wanted more, so I lifted her tiny rayon skirt, as soft to the touch as her goddess skin. It was a glorious encounter with such charm that it could've lasted an eternity without a single complaint on my behalf. I couldn't have enough of her taste and her touch. My own self wasn't as important as her.

Just like the ocean breeze shifts directions, Iris stopped and looked at me differently. Her mood changed back into a mindful being. She stared at me.

"Wait, I think I shouldn't," she said emphatically, convincing herself to halt her desires.

I immediately stopped. I didn't want Iris to feel insecure about her decision to be with me at all. I didn't want to become a regret in her life.

"Ok, if you think this isn't a good idea, maybe we shouldn't do this."

We sat down, both half-naked.

"I promised myself a long time ago that I wouldn't sleep around. I won't do it until there is a commitment, an agreement that we are there for each other both physically and psychologically," Iris explained, something that frankly I was thinking of myself but didn't have the guts or the will to say.

I smiled at her.

"What are you thinking? Tell me!"

Iris didn't understand how hard it was to think while looking at her breasts show themselves behind her black lace bralette. It was nearly impossible to think at all, let alone listen. Her skin was so soft. Her small neckless fell perfectly in between her breasts like it was calling me to dive into them. I took a deep breath and gave Iris her shirt, just to be able to put myself at ease. After thinking about it for a few seconds, I was able to come to an honest conclusion.

"Thinking about it, I actually agree with you."

"Why didn't you say anything?"

"Because it has come to my attention that it's near impossible to say no to you. Now you naked... that's nothing less than an act of triumph."

She laughed the same way she did when a wave ran me over at the National Park. I was starting to love that laugh. It happened when I was a charming fool.

"So, what now?" I inquired, asking for direction on behalf of my hormones.

"Let's think about it, and then we can decide what to do."

This experience was even worse than nothing at all. I had tried the forbidden fruit. I had tasted it and wanted nothing more for the rest of my life. I was hooked.

I said good night to Iris and went to my bedroom to stare at the ceiling fan and not sleep. It went on for days. I couldn't eat. I couldn't think about anything else. My mother's death felt like a distant memory compared to the overpowering desire to be with Iris. We both agreed that this was for the best, but what would change the dynamic? Even if she decided not to touch me intimately ever again, was I still as willing to be with her? These questions kept bugging my mind over and over again.

Iris left early the next day to head to the hospital. I hardly heard her at around 5 am, looking for food and picking things up. When I woke up, all I saw was a dirty dish, a pan with cooked scrambled eggs, and a note that read: "I love you." That was the final straw. I understood what that note meant to me, so I had to call Kevin.

The phone rang several times. I was too eager to wait for him to be available, so I called Vera instead. It was the same to me; we both have known each other for quite a while. I also knew Kevin confided in her every single indiscretion I told him, even if I specifically asked him not to tell anyone.

"Vera! Hey, how are you? Do you have a minute?"

Vera paused for a bit what she was doing.

"Go ahead."

"I love her. I love her, and I don't see myself spending another minute without her. I love her enough to loose myself and feel that I can take over the world. Maybe I love her too much. She has become the only person I need and want." Vera laughed for a few seconds; then I heard Kevin in the back asking her who I was.

"It's Lucca. He's in love, deep."

"Put him on speaker! Let's hear what he has to say!" said Kevin, rushing Vera to open the phone line for him to participate in the conversation.

"Lucca, what is it?" he finally said

"Kevin, I can't sleep. I can't think. I can't eat. I can't even feel anything else but her."

"Well, my friend, you are in love."

"And it's bad, like the worst case I've seen. I can tell by the tone of your voice," said Vera.

"But what do I do?"

"What do you mean?" asked Kevin, clueless about what happened the last time I saw her.

"The night we came back from San José, we got kind of intimate at home," I explained, trying to avoid any details.

"Kind of intimate?" asked Vera as if she needed more information on the subject.

"Anyway, we didn't go far; she told me she wants commitment before having sex."

"What do you think about that?" asked Kevin. I could feel them looking at each other, trying to figure out what she meant by it.

"I think I agree. My hormones don't, but I do!" I explained with some humor, releasing the tension.

"Well, there's only one way to figure this one out: you need to ask her to be your girlfriend!" said Vera, blaming my lack of commitment as the reason why Iris decided not to keep going that night.

"That's the thing; I think I want to ask her to marry me!" I exclaimed, loud and clear as if I needed the world to know.

"What? Why?" asked Kevin, knowing for a fact how difficult marriage could be.

"Kevin! Stop! Be more sensible!" said Vera, who already turned the conversation into a marital argument.

"Guys! I do! I don't want to live without her!"

"I'm serious, why can't you? Let me ask you differently; why do you think she's the one person you need to marry?" asked Kevin.

"She is remarkable. She is heroic and smart. She understands life in a way that I only dream of. I see her, and I ask myself why she wants to be with a person like me. She's brilliant and could singlehandedly take over the world. I have never seen a girl like her. It's almost as if she has a superpower."

There were a few seconds were Kevin and Vera were utterly silent. I'm assuming they were looking at each other, knowing what they were thinking as married couples do.

"Do you like her physically?" asked Vera, realizing I didn't list a single physical attribute.

"I adore her body, her eyes, her hair. Every single thing about her is gorgeous. Have you seen how her hair shines with the sun? Or how her eyes look so deep when she's looking at you?" I tried to explain as if they would understand and have the same opinion of her as I did.

"How long have you been thinking about it?" asked Kevin, who was known for rash decision-making.

"Since our last encounter, four days ago. We have talked every day for hours ever since."

"I'll tell you what; go to the beach today. Sit for a bit and think about it. Try to relax. If tomorrow you still want to go ahead and ask Iris to marry you, then we would help you out," said Vera.

"Sounds like a good plan!" said Kevin. I could hear a high-five over the phone, as always it turned into a team decision.

"Ok, I guess I could do that. But then you guys are in, right?" I confirmed, just making sure they were going to help me successfully propose.

I headed to Manuel Antonio's National Park to clear my head, right where everything started. I went past the beach on the right, through the giant boulder, towards the hidden cove. It was a weekday afternoon, and hardly anyone was as far off the entrance as me. I had the small cove all to myself. So, I sat on some driftwood and looked into the deep blue sea. The sun was bright and gave a sandy brown color to the skies. Maybe the inspiration that emanated from such beautiful landscape would reach into my heart once more to give answers to my questions. Perhaps such striking vegetation would give me the guts to make decisions without feeling consumed by my emotions. Was I really in love with her? Was it her "no" that night that made me feel that I wanted to be with her? Was she in love with me as much as I was with her?

As the waves moved along, and my feet cooled down from the water, I came to the realization that I was afraid more than anything else. I was afraid she wouldn't love me the way I did her. I was terrified about a possible rejection. Most of all I was afraid to not be able to spend the rest of my life with her. She could be old and cranky. Her body could change, her hair could turn gray. It wasn't about my obsession with her body in the end. It was my adoration of her essence. All I needed to know was if she felt the same way about me. All I had to do was ask.

I got my phone in my hand and called her.

She's probably too busy to answer, I thought to myself. It calmed my nerves to think that she wasn't going to answer the phone, at least for a few seconds.

"Lucca? Hi!" said Iris, always happy to hear me.

"Hello my love," I said, as what resided only in my thoughts wanted to become a reality.

She giggled for a bit. Maybe she was excited to hear

me. Maybe it was a nervous laugh. Who knows?

"Hello! What can I do for you, my handsome tico?" She joked around just to break the ice. We could both feel some tension building to become a very serious conversation.

"I was thinking about you," I said, clearing my throat.

"Can I ask you a question?" I continued.

"Sure."

"Why do you love me so? Because in my head, I can list a million things on why I love you, but I don't understand why you love me. I feel I don't deserve you."

There were a few seconds of waiting that became an eternity, and then she said:

"Well, Lucca, it's quite simple. I love you because you're honest with yourself and others. I have never met a person so transparent and easy to understand as you. I love you because you are the most loving person I know. You love people so much that sometimes it becomes a burden for you. I love you because, even though you can be all over the world doing who knows what, you decide to come to your family and be with them. You surround yourself with your little cousins instead of going out with friends. I love you because you are a solid man. You try to do the right thing to the point of your own detriment. I've seen you in your best and still you're humble. I've seen you in your darkest and still you're gentle."

It was the most flattering piece of poetry anyone had ever said to me. She didn't make it dorky or meaningless. She meant every word. She was real. She could see in me things I had never seen in myself. Whenever I made a decision, regardless of how trivial, she was looking. She was paying attention, analyzing, and appreciating. She swept me off my feet.

"Wow, I thought you were going to say I was nice. That was some solid flattery. If you were selling a product, I would totally buy it!" I said to her without thinking.

"Well, the package does help!" she added, just to put the cherry on top.

"Do you want to come by later, maybe?"

"I can't tonight, I have a double shift. But tomorrow I have a day off!"

"Tomorrow it is then."

I was still unsure about the many decisions I had to make in my life. The fear of it all clouded my judgement. Should I sue Ivo the crook to get my property back? Should I ask Iris to marry me, or was I being too hasty about my relationship with her?

CHAPTER XXII

Signed, sealed, delivered

I t was closing time at Manuel Antonio's National Park, so I headed home. I felt defeated because it was my nature to be hard on myself and because I didn't get to solve not even one of the insistent questions in my mind. I sat on the couch, willing to make amends with my present self, whatever the future may hold.

On the coffee table I still had the documents I brought home regarding my new royalty status. So, I grabbed them to safely store them in a more permanent place. As I headed to my bedroom, where most of my belongings were, I noticed the sealed envelope that Jorge gave me as part of my biological father's many documents. I finally got the time and the head to open it, so I walked back to the old couch and opened the letter. The seal, a medieval-looking wax circle with the house code of arms, was so intricate that it got me uneasy to break it, so like the proletariat class I am, I tried opening the letter without breaking the seal, to keep it as a souvenir.

I finally reached its contents by opening the side of the envelope with scissors. Inside there was a very familiar letter.

"I have seen this before," I told myself while moving my eyes right and left, thinking about where I last saw it. Before I even started to read, it came to my mind.

"The tin box!" I said out loud for the whole world to hear. I quickly accessed one of the side tables in the living room, which had an open bottom where I stored the tin box. I opened it as fast as my fat, nail-deprived fingers could and got the unreadable letter that was part of the mysteries in the box.

I compared them, side by side. The letters were identical, with a few clear exceptions. First of all, the letter from the tin box was utterly illegible, with faded characters that hardly amounted to one-fourth of the body of the letter. The rest of the characters weren't even visible. There was also a difference in the paper quality of the writings. The older letter had a rough and inconsistent type of paper, while the letter given to me by Jorge had a simple-looking paper in both color and texture. Jorge was clearly copying the letter over and over again until my biological dad couldn't seal it anymore. That way, he made sure the ancient ink wouldn't be the reason why the letter didn't arrive to its destination. What I was about to read was important. It was so important that it became a matter for a lawyer to get involved. With all the seriousness that entailed this piece of paper, I read, almost like a religious experience.

Alfredo:

As you and I grow older into our dawn, each of us at our own pace, I wanted to let you know a few things as your father and give you some life advice. Yes, you grew up in Costa Rica, where the beaches are pristine and seducing enough for you to stay forever, but if you're reading this letter, chances are you know we aren't authentic Ticos. We emigrated, as you remember, to the fashionable Americas, at the brink of a second world war. We left everything behind, not because your mom and I wanted to have an adventure, but because it was the right thing to do for you. You see, if we stayed, you would have been raised a Nazi, a degenerate and racist human being. The Nazi regime would have taught you that your skin color defines you as a person and that you could judge and discriminate because of race, culture, or religion. You would have learned to hate and identify people in groups and not based on the content of their character. We didn't want you to grow up believing in such things. As parents, we wanted something better, so we looked for a place full of immigrants like us. A place where people traveled to stay when they were tired of titles, races, status, and segregation; an area where we were all the same hard-working people who wanted a future where we could all love each other. We were trying to do the right thing. Often doing the right thing involves sacrifices. Maybe you would sacrifice your safety, maybe your security. Perhaps your fame, or your power, or your money. DO IT NEVERTHELESS. The truth is worth sacrificing for. Maybe you will not bear the fruit of those sacrifices yourself, but your children will, and they will remember that not long ago, their ancestors gave it all. Yes, you will be afraid, but your fear is just a feeling that will pass, even if it takes years. One day your children will know about me, and when they face uncertainty, if you tell them our story, perhaps they would be more inclined to choose wisely.

With love,

Sigismund

As tears filled my eyes, I realized my own quest for meaning had left me meaningless. My struggles, my decisions, were miniscule obstacles compared to what my previous generations had to endure to be able to call a decision a matter of personal preference. My inheritance went way beyond some properties here and there, but it also carried the responsibility of doing what was right, even if it carried with it fear and uncertainty. It wasn't about avoiding consequences, for every decision carried one by definition. It was about choosing the right path and sticking to it regardless of the detrimental effect it could have on our lives. For Sigismund and his family, it involved a tremendous economic disadvantage compared to whoever stayed and favored the Nazi regime. For others, it cost them their lives. Still, they chose to do what was required to carry on through the path of righteousness.

The phone rang, interrupting the internalized lesson my grandfather gave me. It was Kevin, uneasy about the decisions I had to make.

"Hey! what's up?" he casually asked.

"Well, I just read a very revelatory letter from my grandfather, Sigismund."

"Really? I thought we were done with the mysteries from your past!"

"In a way, it was the last unsolved piece of the tin box items."

"Vera! Come here! Lucca just figured out the old letter from the tin box!"

Kevin and Vera were absolutely intrigued by my life, and once again, they not only made me their topic of conversation, but they also did care for my well-being. So, I took the time to read the letter to them, as they both expressed awe and felt dearly each sentence of the letter.

"Wow, that was so deep and beautiful!" said Vera. I could even picture her holding her hands close together to her chest when she gave me her opinion on the matter.

"Sound advice! How do you think it applies to your current circumstances?" asked Kevin, almost parenting me with his question.

"Well, I think I should try to get the property in Escazú back. It's the right thing to do."

We all agreed that contending the property was the right thing to do. I added calling Max as part of my mental checklist to proceed with the process.

"What about your more romantic matters?" asked

Kevin, maybe already making plans on coming to Quepos for the weekend.

"Well, I think she loves me, but asking for her to marry me is selfish on my part. I haven't considered if it's the right time for her to take that big step."

"I can figure that out!" shouted Vera.

"Wait, what?" I asked, not sure of what she meant.

"We've been talking, you know, we are friends. I talked to her yesterday for half an hour!"

Oddly enough, Vera, who was supposed to be my close friend, was apparently Iris's "best Tica friend". This opened a world of information I didn't know I had.

"Well, well, well! You were excessively discreet about it, to say the least!" I said to Vera sarcastically, specially because I felt secretly jealous about me not being her preferred person in the relationship.

"Are you getting jealous about my wife?" Kevin chuckled. It all seemed very amusing for Kevin to witness the fact that I was a bit jealous about Vera's friendship with Iris.

"Vera, do you know something I should know?"

"Oh, many things! Regarding Iris, life..." Vera laughed.

"Vera..." I exponentially increased the tone of my voice, building up to some sort of scolding.

"Lucca, what kind of friend would I be if I tell her about your proposal dilemma? I wouldn't do it to any of you because you're both my friends."

"It's ok. I'll tell you if she spills the beans by mistake. I got you," said Kevin as he declared his loyalty to the house of Prussia.

Honestly, I didn't envy their complex relationships with Iris and me. On the one hand, there was me, family, with all the advantages of a deeply rooted friendship. I could easily suggest my disconformity towards their silence; make them feel bad for not calming my nerves by telling me what Iris confided in them. On the other hand, there was Iris, the vulnerability of a new relationship that can easily fall from grace due to gossip or any other misstep.

As Costa Ricans usually do, we all cracked some jokes to get out of uncomfortable situations. As painful as it was not to know what to do, I had to respect their boundaries. The more I thought about it, the more I understood that I wished to tell her I wanted to spend the rest of my life with her, regardless of the outcome. I was hopeful the answer to my proposal would be positive, but I had to be cautious about my feelings. Nevertheless, I was set. I had decided. I was going to ask Iris to marry me. The hell with fear. Besides, it was more terrifying to see a future without her. I wanted to travel and experience life with her. I wanted to have a family and grow old with her. I even wanted to sit on the couch and watch TV with her instead of by myself.

CHAPTER XXIII

But my life, my love, and my lady is the sea

As my next step, I decided to go to Esterillos Beach to watch some surfing amid the sunset. I was beginning to have a lifestyle change. A few weeks ago, I would have never thought to jump from one beach to another according to my mood. But here I was, feeling the need for beach activity right after leaving a solitary beach. Esterillos Beach is the right place to be part of the community. With their traditional boats or pangas, fishermen park their colorful vessels throughout the beach, making it a very quaint little detail to a scenic view. I parked myself close to one of the vessels, right on the sand. The turquoise boat called Pilo had an interesting design, and a similar owner whose tanned skin from the sun could almost make a cracking sound when it moved. He was slowly going back and forth with some seafood that he carried from the boat. Contrary to the rest of the beach population at the time, I was still and alone, which made him curious enough to get close to me, looking for a chat.

He sat there, as steady as me, as if we were the oldest of friends, with an oyster in one hand and a knife in the other, as he opened the oyster.

"Hello there, *Mae*! *Pura Vida*?" Maybe he saw in me what resembled a hyper-thoughtful man, with my frowning forehead and my sight deep as the ocean in front of me.

"Hi! *Pura Vida*!" I answered his question with a half-smile, almost as if half of my face couldn't celebrate my new acquaintance.

"I'm the perfect stranger that you would probably never meet again, so, tell me, what is making you look at the sea with such contempt?"

I laughed at the audacity of his comment. It didn't surprise me, though; Ticos are extra-caring; they don't mind exchanging discomfort for care. His gray hair occasionally danced with the ocean breeze, and his big belly hardly made the fitted fisherman's stereotype believable. His knife made a crackling sound as he inserted it in the oyster, a motion he was visibly a veteran at performing.

"I'm deciding if I want to marry a girl," I told

him. He paused his butchering moves through the oyster for a second. He then turned to me and said:

"Do you see all those surfers riding the waves up and down? See how they look as if they were born at sea rather than on land?" He pointed at the one surfer, riding his wave with a white surfing board. A veteran at his own craft as well, one could notice because of how he fixed his hair and played with his body; the balancing act he was performing was second nature to him.

"Yes."

"Well, they didn't sit down to think about if they wanted to surf. They just saw a board that looked interesting enough, picked it up, and started to practice until they didn't have to make an effort." I thought for a few seconds about what he said to figure out the meaning of the analogy. He cut my thoughts short and said:

"Relationships are the same way. You picked a girl you found you could love for life. Now the question is: Do you want to pick up the board and ride the wave, or would you rather sit here and see someone else ride the wave for you? The question is, rather: Do you really want to surf?"

I looked at him perplexed; not every day you find a random guy to be a personal guru in favor of your cause.

"Boy! Do you want to be married?" he finally told me since I was proven too slow to deduct his meaning.

"I don't mind the married part, as long as it is the right person."

"What's keeping you from it, then?"

"Well, first, I need a ring. I have my late mother's, but my girl took care of her while in the hospital where she died. I don't want to give her a ring she saw on a dead patient of hers."

He laughed with his belly while finally opening the oyster.

"I thought your situation was a bit more philosophical than looking for a ring... Let's see...," He thought for a second as he opened the oyster wide. From inside, you could see a tiny pearl, pearlescent enough to catch a glimpse of the sun. The fisherman grabbed the pearl with his left hand and showed it to me.

"What if you change the stone for something more local?" he said.

My eyes widened, reacting to what I thought was a magnificent idea. After all, it was here in Costa Rica where we fell in love.

"You're a genius! Where do I get one?"

"Well, how about you come with me tomorrow morning, 5 a.m.? We could ride together, and I'll teach you to fish for a one-of-a-kind pearl. Then you can go to the local jeweler and ask them to mount it on top of your mother's ring!"

The early morning suggestion made me hesitate for a bit, but then I agreed to his proposal. I was going to be such a hit! I was going to the bottom of the ocean, to the beach of our dreams, to get Iris a pearl for her engagement ring! Hopefully, this random dude wasn't the dangerous type. Maybe I should buy a knife also, just in case. He was a local, so it was easy enough to figure out who he was, just to be on the safe side.

The next day came, and I was ready to take a deep dive into the ocean for the sake of my special lady. The excitement of a new experience confused itself with fear of rejection. Nevertheless, I went forward with the plan as a decisive soldier about to confront war (if my grandfather heard my thoughts, he would probably roll out of his grave).

I arrived at the beach, nothing but five minutes late, and the fisherman was already on his boat about to head out.

"Hey, wait up!" I yelled from a distance, afraid he

might leave me behind.

"There he is! Finally! I thought you weren't coming!" The fisherman laughed.

"*Pura Vida!*" I replied while lifting my chin a bit as a salutation.

"Hurry, come on in! I'm Pilo," he said while cleaning his hand dry and extending it to shake mine. He was already busy lifting the anchor.

"Lucca!" I replied while shaking his hand.

His eyes widened:

"Are you Aura's son?" It was surprising to me to see how many people were connected to my life in one way or another. Perfect strangers had a connection to my life without me even knowing.

"Yes! Did you know her?" I asked. Honestly, I was breathing a little lighter, thinking that it wasn't a perfect stranger who would be in charge of the vessel anymore. Now that I knew he somewhat met me before, it was a breath of fresh air. I could be a little more trusting since he was automatically more liable to the community.

"Do I know her? *Chavalo!* I know you!" he said, smiling at the coincidence of the casual encounter.

He seemed to always be laughing and in a

good mood. Maybe it was the amount of sunlight he received every day, producing an extreme dose of vitamin D, which meant more happy chemicals. Perhaps it was the simplicity of a lifestyle that was as obsolete as it was unreachable for many. Without knowing, he was a species on the brink of extinction. There was no social media that made him angry at the world around him. There wasn't any performance stress from an insatiable boss. It was only him and the sea, with its occasional storm. Nothing else to complicate life. No extreme decision-making. No rush hour. No competitive environment. Maybe he was the one living in luxury more than I was!

"From where?" My consternation was insisting on an answer from his implication.

"Lucca, I used to bring your mom fresh seafood right after my early catch. Sometimes you were there, bugging her arm or asking for attention in any possible form. You were a needy child, if you ask me."

Great. . . I thought to myself, *Now my partner in crime feels I'm just a spoiled kid. I'm going to have to show him that it's not the case anymore.*

I smiled politely while I set my backpack on the boat's floor. Then we both hopped out of the *panga* to push it into the water. The waves, as small as they were, were difficult to fight against. They pushed the boat out hard with every hit, making it a very intentional effort to try to navigate the sea. It was almost as if the sea was telling us to stay away from it, like a fierce cat that pushes caressing hands away.

Pilo hopped in as effortlessly as a cowboy mounting a horse. He then extended his hand and pulled me in.

"Ready to get a treasure for your girl?" he asked.

"Ready, captain!" I said, to get into the maritime mood we both expected from the trip.

Off we went, all dependent on a small motor attached to the vessel. God forbid the loosely attached machine failed in the middle of the sea.

The trip was pleasant. The breeze hit my face with a salty scent so strong it invaded my taste buds. Although thick and short, my wavy hair played along with the wind as the boat moved forth with speed. The experience itself belonged to a wanderlust dream until we stopped to get into our diving gear. Then the waves tossed us up and down... over and over again. The beauty of the sea became a seasick nightmare. My head began to spin. I couldn't find my ground for obvious reasons. I got disoriented and confused. My stomach followed the trap as it churned acids due to nausea. It was all moving.

"Lucca, you look a little sick. You need to get off the boat to feel less movement," suggested Pilo, a prominent veteran at sea who had clearly seen my reaction before.

I kept putting on my gear to get out of the boat as fast as I could. Pilo put his hand on my arm, stopping my movement.

"You can't dive with nausea, Lucca. You might drown if you throw up." I guess it showed my inexperience at sea. I spent all my youth in and out of surfboards, but I never tried diving. "You're too young to dive," my mom would say every time I asked. Kevin never dived either since my mom was his caretaker while staying in Quepos.

"Don't worry. I'll get a pearl for you. It will be our secret." Pilo winked as if he had a plan B all along.

I stayed at surface level and used my very rudimentary snorkel gear to watch from afar what Pilo picked. Pilo, well over his 50s, took a deep breath but no gear at all to dive. The astonishing sight made me peek overboard, only to realize that he never packed two sets of diving gear at all. I guess he just wanted some new company for his diving expedition. It was interesting how he would take a big gulp of air and move into the deep, sometimes well beyond 16 feet. It was second nature to him. He carried a small net that got filled up with more and more oysters until he eventually carried around 60 mollusks with him. He also got some other species used to make traditional plates, like *cambute*, which is illegal to sell in Costa Rica due to its slow but steady path towards extinction. He would only get one every month for his mom to cook the traditional meal. We climbed up the boat and headed back to shore as fast as we could, Pilo probably fearing my seasick self throwing up in his vessel.

As pale as I probably looked from the sea not getting along with my stomach, I was a happy camper with my newly acquired unforgettable memory. Pilo was just getting started on his full-time job, which included preparing and selling his product to neighbors and businesses. Right at the beach, he had a little shack made of four posters and a dried-palm rooftop, where he had all the ingredients already prepared by his family. I helped him frantically, maybe out of guilt due to my underperformance. After all, I was still trying to earn my precious pearl for my beautiful girl.

Pilo slowly grabbed his faithful companion, the knife he previously used to open mollusks when we first talked to each other. One by one, Pilo opened each oyster with immaculate precision but with a fast-paced rhythm. He saw me staring at his work, so he offered me a try.

It was a bit overwhelming to feel the

life of an animal taken away by my hand. At first, one feels like you're breaking some sort of code, some people even stop there. They feel too uncomfortable with the situation. I was taught by my father not to be scared by the act of taking away life to eat. *"If you forget where your food comes from and how difficult it is to bring it to the table, you become self-entitled and disconnected with your condition as a human being,"* he used to say. So, we did some fishing and had chickens at home. I even remember my dad asking me to help him kill a chicken for a Christmas dinner. I guess he was kind of right. People nowadays go to grocery stores to get their food and have no idea what a farmer or a fisherman had to endure to sell that product.

I successfully opened the oyster and looked at him as a child whose father is about to be proud of them.

"There you go! You're almost there! After a bit of practice, you would be able to do what I do! Soon we'll see a little panga boat called *The Lucca* parked at the beach!" I couldn't tell if he was encouraging me or mocking my inexperience. I honestly didn't care. He was kind enough to offer me a ride and patient enough to bring me to shore prematurely.

I handed him the knife, and he kept opening the oysters. What appeared to be his oldest child had the production line memorized by heart; he was already squeezing mandarin lemons, the locals' favorite type for ceviche, into a bowl.

"We got a winner!" shouted Pilo as he opened one of the last oysters from his net.

He immediately got a round, black pearl the size of a pea from the oyster. He showed me the pearl, his chunky fingers holding it steady against the sunlight.

"See how it's pearlescent, just like the oyster's mother-of-pearl interior coat?"

I got closer to appreciate the effect.

"Yes! It looks fantastic!"

"That means it's a natural pearl and not some cultivated counterfeit," Pilo said, a bit bitter at the number of cultured pearls that are now seizing the market due to its low prices.

We chatted as the oyster *ceviche* cooked itself in lemon juice, as fresh as it comes and as natural as it could be. It was delicious; the purple onion and red pepper added great flavor to it, and the cilantro's final touch combined the earthy taste of the plant with the salty taste of the ocean.

After the *ceviche*, I helped him set up for his sale, and then gave him some financial retribution for a priceless experience and a memorable souvenir.

We shook hands, and I parted ways back to the house. I called Kevin on the way to let him and Vera know that I was able to acquire the pearl. Kevin was already heading to Quepos to help me plan an unforgettable proposal. I was reluctantly missing my mom. I tried to ignore the fact that a person's life changes drastically once a mother dies. She would have been the first one to make plans and get creative with the idea. Iris would have gotten along with her so well. She probably would have learned how to get around the area so much better with her.

CHAPTER XXIV

Take a chance on me

Kevin and Vera arrived late at night. They came without their kids, ready to create an unforgettable proposal for Iris. That day was a beautiful December day, the month with the most colorful sunsets and the best breeze. The northern winds, as the Ticos call them, bring with them cooler, dryer weather. It makes the beach have an ideal temperature and the most color during sunsets. I woke to the sound of breakfast. Kevin, who I already trusted with my life more than once, had a spare copy of the house's keys. Vera was still sleeping; her conflict with life had always been with the early mornings. On the other hand, Kevin was up and running at 7:00 a.m. sometimes with a too cheerful attitude.

"My man!" said Kevin as soon as he saw me.

With his very cool walking rhythm, Kevin was preparing himself for a hug from where he was standing right at the other end of the hall. Anyone watching us would have bet we hadn't seen each other in ages. Looking back, I could guess he was probably excited about my plans with Iris. His reaction reminded me I still had a family to belong to, a support system, a base where I could take refuge during turbulent times.

He came to meet me at the hall like if we hadn't seen each other in ages. He smiled and hugged me with an honest embrace. He was already thinking about my huge next step, I could tell.

"Hey, Kevin! Are you ready to rock Iris's world?" I said, knowing for a fact that he was enjoying the experience the most out of all of us. I was too nervous to agree with his pleasant attitude.

"Well, have a seat, let's talk about your plans," said Kevin while cooking some *huevos rancheros*. The whole Central America region cooks *huevos rancheros*, but no plate is the same. Some add spicy peppers; some only add bell pepper and onions to scrambled eggs. The family recipe dictates for scrambled eggs, diced tomato, onions, and chicken bouillon. Kevin's eggs are delicious because he undercooks the eggs a bit, just enough to make them juicy.

"Well, maybe we can go to Manuel Antonio's National Park since our whole romance spurred from there," I suggested, considering Iris's pragmatic personality. She wouldn't appreciate a loud encounter full of attention. She was more even-tempered than such bombastic ideas.

"Simple and meaningful, I like it!"

"Sounds like a plan," said Vera from behind while brushing her teeth. She had just woken up, probably from the scent of scrambled eggs. If there's something Vera likes more than sleeping, is eating. Her curly hair was a little messed up from her recent pillow encounter.

"What can we help you with?" asked Kevin, already serving the delicious meal on our respective dishes.

"Well, the jewelry store is going to have the ring ready today, but I'm already with Iris when that happens, so maybe you can pick it up for me?"

"Sure, just give me the address and receipt; we'll take care of the rest!"

With that I retreated to the living room and called Iris. I wanted to make sure she was able to make it before the closing of Manuel Antonio's National Park.

"Hello, Lucca! Long time no see!" she teased. In reality, Iris and I were texting long into the night.

"Hello, my love. Did you have a good night?" I asked her. She loved me calling her *my love*. The expression in English sounds like something right out of a cheesy eighteenth-century drama, but in Spanish, it was a common way to call a person. For Iris, it meant I was extra romantic and a Latino. Both attributes were a reason for pride in her conversations with her friends. She also made the remark once of how the word *honey* is so overused by couples, turning it into a meaningless expression. For Iris, *my love* was extra; it required effort and a conscientious decision to express love. On the other hand, I was called *my love* by my mother, my aunt, the random lady at the cafeteria. . . In fact, by any person of the opposite sex that was old enough to be my mother. It reminded me of home, and it reminded her she was extra loved by her Latin lover.

"It's impossible to have a good night when my mind is still thinking about you, Lucca." She laughed, making sure I understood her naughtiness behind the comment. She loved to show me her love with words that took some extra seconds to get. I guess intelligent people tend to make funny remarks in such a way. She didn't know I was with Kevin and Vera back at the house, so all Kevin saw from the kitchen was my very red face standing in the living room. I was in trouble. If I didn't respond accordingly, she was going to know I had someone home. I didn't have time to think, so I panicked.

"Yes, great idea! So see you this afternoon, don't forget! Bye!"

What an idiot. I couldn't even pretend I was alone to keep the plan together. I hung up and looked at Kevin and Vera, both in the kitchen, looking at me as some sort of incompetent bureaucrat.

"Why didn't you just say something less awkward! She's going to get suspicious!" Vera scolded me with a smile that could easily translate to embarrassment in different circumstances.

"I don't know! She got private with me, and you guys were here! I panicked!" I complained to them.

After a few seconds, Vera's phone rang. Vera, already suspecting whose call it was, looked at me with one eyebrow up and whispered "*I told you so*" while she headed to pick up the phone.

"Hello! Iris! How are you! How's Quepos!" answered Vera while rolling her eyes back at me.

Kevin found the whole situation amusing and was holding his laugh for the sake of the call.

"Yeah! Sure! What's up?" continued Vera, as she headed to a more private area out on the balcony.

Kevin and I headed to the kitchen window, like we were running for our lives. We knew since we were little that if you open the window right on top of the sink, one could hear the conversations going on on the balcony. Renzo and I figured out Dad was sick that way. Kevin realized his parents were on bad terms one day. We learned a lot about life that way.

"I don't think he has anyone in there, Iris. Lucca is absolutely in love with you. He talks about you constantly," said Vera, reassuring Iris that I wasn't sleeping around.

After some ten minutes Vera hung up and headed inside to give us an update.

"Lucca, you idiot! Now she thinks you have someone in here! I had to tell her I was heading here so she would think you were unwilling!"

"See, Lucca, the thing about smart women is that they can see trouble coming a mile away. Sometimes it's wonderful. Sometimes you end up reprimanded for something that could have happened!" Kevin chuckled.

"Great..." I said sarcastically. "Should I call her again?" I asked while getting my phone.

"No!" Kevin and Vera screamed. I stopped immediately. Apparently, it was already a consensus that it was a bad idea. So, I slowly put my phone down while looking at them in disbelief. I almost felt like the phone was a weapon, and I was supposed to surrender and show my hands.

We kept planning the little details of the proposal: the wine, the glasses, the beach throw, the cooler, the food. We went shopping at the local grocery store downtown, where we coincidentally met Pilo and his enormous family.

"Hey! Pilo!" I yelled to Pilo, who was distracted with the produce section. The whole grocery store looked at me before he noticed, so much so that even a random stranger whistled to make sure oblivious Pilo looked back at me.

"Lucca! How are you? Did the ring turn out looking fancy?" he asked with a sense of pride.

"I haven't seen it yet, but I promise to take my future fiancée to Esterillos so you can see the ring for yourself."

"Aww!" Three of his daughters sighed at the romantic idea that for sure the whole family knew by now–yes, there were more than three daughters present.

"When are you proposing?" asked one of the girls.

"This afternoon, at Manuel Antonio, before the closing of the park," I told the tween girl who seemed to be the most interested in the story.

"Today? Oh, man, good luck! Make it unforgettable! If you need any more help, just call me!" Pilo said while writing his number on an old receipt he had in his pocket.

By then, it was already midday; the mental countdown had begun. Iris and I decided to meet at Manuel Antonio, which worked great for my plan. I carefully packed a picnic basket and a cooler so it wouldn't be so obvious I had special plans. It was going to be great. The beach, in its customary splendor, was going to be the background of a hell of a love story. The sand and the sea were going to be complicit in this conspiracy in favor of love. The birds would be the soundtrack vocals; the leaves of the trees, the percussion. There was no fancy dress or shoes. Just us and the fantastic landscape of this delightful paradise I luckily could call home.

At least that's what I imagined.

The reality of the situation was very different, though. As agreed, we decided to meet there, a little earlier than Kevin and Vera's arrival. Iris was enjoying the sun. I was in absolute agony over my immediate future. I wished Iris didn't suspect a thing, but being the mind reader she was, she kept looking at me with suspicion. Finally, Kevin texted me that he had arrived at the park, so I excused myself from whatever fun we were having and headed to the restrooms, where we would meet to finish the ring transaction.

"Ok, Lucca, here it is! Are you sure about this? After you ask, it would be a little more difficult to back down from a wedding!" said Kevin with his hand on my shoulder. I felt as if I had a big brother who had my back.

"I'm positive," I told Kevin with a persistent tone. I wanted him to know I was more sure of this decision than any other decision in my life.

"Here you go then," said Kevin, handing me a little purple ring box, velvet lined in and out. The ring looked gorgeous. An old, white gold ring had been transformed into this unique, priceless piece of art. The different curves that before didn't resemble much were now clearly vines, almost Celtic looking, that surrounded the pearl, held in between its leaves. It was magnificent and one of a kind. Mom would have been amazed at the transformation.

"Oh, wow!" I expressed to Kevin as I opened the box.

"It looks like something out of a fairy tale!" said Vera from the back. She was busy setting up the camera to capture the moment.

I put the ring inside my pocket and walked back to

the beach where Iris was waiting for me.

"How did it go? Are they far?" said Iris, still thinking I was using the restrooms at the National Park.

"Oh, yes! You better take your time if you want to get there!" I nervously suggested. I had realized by now I was a terrible liar. Hopefully, the colossal oddness I was bringing to the table wouldn't be too evident for Iris.

We sat on the beach, my legs shaky from the nerves. I was sweating like crazy, and it wasn't even a hot afternoon. I tried to pretend I was hyperactive that day so Iris would miss my anxiety.

I was finally able to relax a bit, when suddenly I saw a turquoise boat right in front of us, with a big, white sign made out of some sort of soft material that said: "*SAI JES*". A small figure from a distance jumped up and down and moved his arms around.

It finally hit me: it was Pilo! I could tell by his belly and his gray hair. He was rocking with the sea, holding what looked like a glass bottle. *Oh, no!* I thought. He was clearly drunk, noticeable by the way his body balanced with the sea. He kept falling from the movement of the waves, something he wouldn't do unless he was drunk.

"What's that person out in the open doing? Is he in trouble?" asked Iris, always looking to help. Not very convenient at this moment.

"'SAI JES' I wonder who Jes is... He probably forgot the second 's' or something," Iris deduced from the sight.

I was so concerned about Iris digging into Pilo's misbehavior that I placed the ring box on top of the beach throw without thinking about it twice. I immediately grabbed her and turned her around for her not to see him make a fool of himself and give away the surprise.

She got startled at the forced movement, and my own strength made her fall to the sand. We were sitting close to the palm trees to avoid too much afternoon sun exposure. We thought we were cautious, but the truth was very different. The monkeys, who were minding my business, suddenly dropped from the palm tree and immediately went for the little, flashy purple item on the floor. I saw everything in slow motion: the monkey grabbing the engagement ring box, me trying to apologize to Iris for tossing her to the sand like some sort of disposable object, and Kevin, who was hiding with Vera to record the incident, jumped out of the trees yelling "Noooooo!!!!!"

He tried to grab the mischievous monkey

from the leg. The monkey already felt the chase too close to him, so he jumped back to his base: a tall palm tree hanging from one of the mountain skirts that touched the sea. Kevin, who never knew when to stop, followed the monkey like some maniac. The monkey felt threatened, so he climbed higher and higher to the top of the palm tree. Kevin kept following. Vera kept filming.

"Oh, well, this WILL be memorable for sure!"

"Wait, what's going on? Why are Kevin and Vera here with you? Why were they hiding in the bushes?" Iris asked, trying to analyze the situation.

"Don't think about it too much; we were just pulling a prank!" I said with a nervous smile. And then, as my anxious self always does, I kept talking nonsense.

"Kevin! Watch out! You're kind of too high up!" said Vera.

Kevin instinctively looked down due to Vera's remark and closed his eyes.

"I'm way too high! I don't think I can get off!"

"Lucca, the guy with the Jes sign just fell from his boat! Is he ok?" said Iris, still clueless about the proposal. Probably not for long.

Vera glanced at the ocean to take a look at

what Iris was setting her eyes on.

"Wait, isn't that your friend Pilo?" she said without any regard to the secret between us. I guess by then, the whole event went crashing down, and we were basically in the damage control phase of the proposal.

"Do you know that guy? Who's Pilo? I haven't met him, have I?" asked Iris, already connecting the dots from the catastrophe.

I looked back, and of course, the drunk Pilo fell from his panga, so I decided to head to the ocean to see if he was conscious enough to breathe underwater.

"The monkey, it let go of the ring!" yelled Kevin, too terrified to try to keep facts from Iris.

"Wait, a ring? Lucca, a ring?" Finally, Iris understood the secrecy behind it all.

"Oh my God! Look at how Pilo wrote 'say yes,' Kevin! Can you see from up there?" Vera called to Kevin.

"Say yes! Of course!"

"Wait, does that mean yes to the proposal, or are you just reading the sign?" yelled Kevin from the top.

"Kevin, can you try to get off, or are we past that point?" asked Vera, still concerned for Kevin.

"Let me see… Nope, stuck as this palm tree!"

Iris, understanding that Kevin might be in danger if he let go, called 911 to ask for support.

"Vera! Did you get the ring?! It's down there somewhere! The monkey let go of the box!" Vera immediately got closer to the area where the tip of the palm tree bent and could spot the small, purple box in the middle of some debris.

"Got it!"

"Great! Now, who's going to get me!" asked Kevin, eyes shut, grabbing that palm tree as if he was hugging Vera for one last time.

I was already coming out of the water, soaking wet. I didn't make it halfway when Pilo yelled:

"I'm ok!" And climbed back to his vessel like nothing really happened.

Iris looked at me. She let go a little giggle from the whole experience.

"Lucca, my love, were you about to pop the big question?"

I looked down, embarrassed by my failure.

I recognized I wasn't the same man that started this journey. I wasn't mad at life for bringing some unpredictabilities into my plans. I wasn't stressed from the unexpected outcome. I wasn't having a tantrum because my very thoughtful arrangements didn't turn out to be even a bit close to the actual result. I was completely and utterly fine with it. I was able to look at the situation as a third person, almost as if it happened to someone else. Because of this new perspective, my feelings weren't taking over. My mind wasn't going a thousand miles per hour. I was able to think about what to say and do because my brain could work to its total capacity to solve problems. My anxiety wasn't robbing me of brain power. I guess I grew up a little that day.

So, with soaking clothes and all, I bent one knee, looked Iris in the eye, and said:

"Iris, as you can see, I'm not the perfect man, not even close. But you know my weaknesses and my strengths. You are also the strongest, most incomparably smart and giving person I know. Now, the question is: Do you want to surf life's waves with me for better or worse?"

She looked at me, seriously thinking about it, as I thought she would. Vera was already handing me the ring from behind.

"Well, there are some things we need to do first,

but I think we can commit to each other right away. After all, there's no one in the world I'd rather be with."

Iris's eyes sparkled like two dark, shiny marbles. She grabbed my face with one hand, and I opened the ring and placed it on her tiny finger as the sound of the firefighter sirens got closer and closer. Vera was taking pictures like crazy while she sporadically looked up into the palm tree to make sure her husband was still alive. I playfully pulled Iris down to the sand and kissed her while she was resting in my arms.

"We received a call that a subject is stuck in a tree from pursuing a monkey?" said a voice from behind. Vera stopped taking pictures and pointed at Kevin.

"There he is! He was trying to be a hero but failed!" said Vera, almost laughing at poor Kevin. She went on ahead with the firefighters to take pictures of her husband's descent for her family album.

We sat together on the sand, laughing at the whole experience. My mother used to laugh a lot when things went wrong. Sometimes it annoyed me, so I asked her once why.

"Because it's better to laugh than to cry!" she would say. At that moment, I understood why.

After a half hour rescue operation that looked more like a circus act, Kevin was finally able to come down from the palm tree back to safety. After making sure he was still in one piece, he congratulated us on our new engagement.

We all decided the afternoon proved exhausting, so we headed back to the car. After arriving at the vehicle, I noticed I didn't have my flip-flops on; I walked barefoot the whole time without noticing.

"My shoes!" I said to everyone who was already closing the car doors to head home.

"Do you need to go back and look for them?" asked Iris.

I thought for a second. A month ago, I would've been so mad about leaving my shoes. But now, I didn't care.

"Nah! It's ok. If I didn't notice before, why bother now!" I said, completely carefree.

That's what Costa Rica does to you. It turns control freaks and nervous wrecks into carefree human beings. That's the power of community and nature. That's the magic of this place. It's not only about the cool pictures to post on social media, or the new experiences to tell your kids as you grow old. It changes your soul. It makes you a better version of yourself. It absorbs what made you a machine, and it exchanges it for a decent person. A person that can genuinely say "Pura Vida" and understand that life can indeed be pure. My troubles aren't over, and that's the way it is going to be for as long as any of us live. Ivo is still out there trying to steal my properties. My mom is still gone. My German side of the family doesn't know I exist. But nothing matters as much as living with peace of mind and a full heart. My grandfather was right about moving to Costa Rica after all.

ACKNOWLEDGEMENTS

What happens when you mix being homesick with a case of depression? Well, you write. You write until either you feel you're a terrible writer and stop writing altogether, or you feel you're a horrible writer all the same, but you keep going because it feeds your soul. Either way, the feeling that you don't like your penmanship doesn't go away, but there are a few selected individuals who support you no matter how horrendous you think you write.

First, I want to thank my mother for choosing to give me a quality education above all else. As a single mother with a low-income background, she insisted I be enrolled in a demanding school in Costa Rica to prove the point that education matters. Thank you for believing in me and not giving up regardless of the distress in your life. Furthermore, thank you for not only allowing but also encouraging my imagination to run wild. It made the difference, and now I can imagine stories, characters, and landscapes because of it.

Second, I want to thank my son Samuel and my daughter Priscilla for being my inspiration. I wouldn't have written this without you. I also want to thank them for being my unofficial editors, which brings me to my next acknowledgement _to all the high-school teachers out there: thank you. Sometimes as educators, you might find yourselves tired of fighting against attitudes from staff or students, but believe me, what you teach, and the excellence of your work truly makes a difference.

I also want to thank my husband of 20+ years, Roy, whose engineering background suggests the kind of sacrifice he had to make to read this book several times and give his honest opinion. I know you would rather watch quantum physics documentaries, so thank you.

Finally, I want to thank my editor Judi Weiss, and the countless friends and family members that read this book and wished me the best. Thank you for your support, your enthusiasm, and every opportunity you gave me to show my work.

To all struggling writers out there, this one is for you!

Follow me online and on social media!

www.ella-vega.com

@ellavegaauthor

ellavegaauthor.com

Cover design by Gabriela Reyes

Printed in Great Britain
by Amazon